IDAHO
ICE
BEAST

Here's what readers from around the country are saying about Johnathan Rand's AMERICAN CHILLERS:

"MISSISSIPPI MEGALODON was awesome! You're the best writer in the WORLD!"

-Julian T., age 8, Florida

"American Chillers is the best book series in the world! I love them!"

-Anneliese B., age 10, Michigan

"I'm reading FLORIDA FOG PHANTOMS, and it's great! When are you going to write a book about Utah?"

-David H., Age 7, Utah

"MISSISSIPPI MEGALODON is so rad! Where in the world do you get these ideas? You are the awesomest author ever!"

-Eli L., Age 9, Illinois

"I read DANGEROUS DOLLS OF DELAWARE and it was super creepy. My favorite book is POLTERGEISTS OF PETOSKEY. You make me like to read even more!"

-Brendon P., Age 8, Michigan

"I love your books! I just finished SINISTER SPIDERS OF SAGINAW. It really freaked me out! Now I'm reading MISSISSIPPI MEGALODON. It's really good. Can you come to our school?"

-Blane B., age 11, Indiana

"I'm your biggest fan in the world! I just started your DOUBLE THRILLERS and it's great!"

-Curtis J., Age 11, California

"I just read the book: CURSE OF THE CONNECTICUT COYOTES and it really freaked me out when Erica thought she got attacked by a coyote!"

-Shaina B., Age 10, Minnesota

"I love your books so much that I read everyone in my school library and public library! I hope I get a chance to come to CHILLERMANIA, and I'm saving my money to make it happen. You rock! Keep writing, and I'm your biggest fan!"

-Makayla B., Age 9, Missouri

"Your books are the best I've ever read in my life! I've read over 20 and double thumbs up to all of them!"

-Justus K., Age 11, California

"I never like to read until I discovered your books. The first one I read was VIRTUAL VAMPIRES OF VERMONT, and it totally freaked me out! Me and my friends have our own American Chillers book club. Will you come to one of our meetings?"

-Carson C., age 12, Oklahoma

"I love the American Chillers series I only have three more books to go! My favorite book is HAUNTING IN NEW HAMPSHIRE. It's awesome!"

-Eriana S., age 10, Ohio

"I've read most of your American Chillers books! My favorite was WISCONSIN WEREWOLVES. Right now I am reading KENTUCKY KOMODO DRAGONS. I love it because it is mystery/adventure/chillers! Thank you for writing such exciting books!"

-Maya R., age 9, Georgia

"When we visited my grandparents in San Diego, I found your books at *The Yellow Book Road* bookstore. I bought one and read it in three days! My grandparents took me back to the bookstore and bought me five more! I can't stop reading them!"

-Amber Y, age 11, Hawaii

"I've read every single one of your Michigan and American Chillers and they're all great! I just finished VICIOUS VACUUMS OF VIRGINIA and I think it's the best one yet! Go Johnathan Rand!"

-Avery R., age 10, Delaware

"Your books are the best ones I've ever read! I tried to write my own, but it's hard! How do you come up with so many great books? Please tell me so I can be a writer, too!"

-Lauren H., age 12, Montana

"My family and I were vacationing in northern Michigan and stopped at CHILLERMANIA and you were there! It was the best day of my life!"

-Andrew T., age 8, Tennessee

Got something cool to say about Johnathan Rand's books? Let us know, and we might publish it right here! Send your short blurb to:

Chiller Blurbs
281 Cool Blurbs Ave.
Topinabee, MI 49791

Other books by Johnathan Rand:

Michigan Chillers:

#1: Mayhem on Mackinac Island
#2: Terror Stalks Traverse City
#3: Poltergeists of Petoskey
#4: Aliens Attack Alpena
#5: Gargoyles of Gaylord
#6: Strange Spirits of St. Ignace
#7: Kreepy Klowns of Kalamazoo
#8: Dinosaurs Destroy Detroit
#9: Sinister Spiders of Saginaw
#10: Mackinaw City Mummies
#11: Great Lakes Ghost Ship
#12: AuSable Alligators
#13: Gruesome Ghouls of Grand Rapids
#14: Bionic Bats of Bay City

American Chillers:

#1: The Michigan Mega-Monsters
#2: Ogres of Ohio
#3: Florida Fog Phantoms
#4: New York Ninjas
#5: Terrible Tractors of Texas
#6: Invisible Iguanas of Illinois
#7: Wisconsin Werewolves
#8: Minnesota Mall Mannequins
#9: Iron Insects Invade Indiana
#10: Missouri Madhouse
#11: Poisonous Pythons Paralyze Pennsylvania
#12: Dangerous Dolls of Delaware
#13: Virtual Vampires of Vermont
#14: Creepy Condors of California
#15: Nebraska Nightcrawlers
#16: Alien Androids Assault Arizona
#17: South Carolina Sea Creatures
#18: Washington Wax Museum
#19: North Dakota Night Dragons
#20: Mutant Mammoths of Montana
#21: Terrifying Toys of Tennessee
#22: Nuclear Jellyfish of New Jersey
#23: Wicked Velociraptors of West Virginia
#24: Haunting in New Hampshire
#25: Mississippi Megalodon
#26: Oklahoma Outbreak
#27: Kentucky Komodo Dragons
#28: Curse of the Connecticut Coyotes
#29: Oregon Oceanauts
#30: Vicious Vacuums of Virginia
#31: The Nevada Nightmare Novel
#32: Idaho Ice Beast

Freddie Fernortner, Fearless First Grader:

#1: The Fantastic Flying Bicycle
#2: The Super-Scary Night Thingy
#3: A Haunting We Will Go
#4: Freddie's Dog Walking Service
#5: The Big Box Fort
#6: Mr. Chewy's Big Adventure
#7: The Magical Wading Pool
#8: Chipper's Crazy Carnival
#9: Attack of the Dust Bunnies from Outer Space!
#10: The Pond Monster
#11: Tadpole Trouble

Adventure Club series:

#1: Ghost in the Graveyard
#2: Ghost in the Grand
#3: The Haunted Schoolhouse

For Teens:

PANDEMIA: A novel of the bird flu and the end of the world
(written with Christopher Knight)

American Chillers Double Thrillers:

Vampire Nation &
Attack of the Monster Venus Melon

**#32: Idaho
Ice
Beast**

Johnathan Rand

PUBLIC LIBRARY

JUN 2012

SOUTH BEND, INDIANA

An AudioCraft Publishing, Inc. book

This book is a work of fiction. Names, places, characters and incidents are used fictitiously, or are products of the author's very active imagination.

Book storage and warehouses provided by Chillermania!©
Indian River, Michigan

No part of this publication may be reproduced in whole or in part, or stored in a retrieval system, or transmitted in any form or by any means, electronic, mechanic, photocopying, recording, or otherwise, without written permission from the publisher. For information regarding permission, write to: AudioCraft Publishing, Inc., PO Box 281, Topinabee Island, MI 49791

American Chillers #32: Idaho Ice Beast
ISBN 13-digit: 978-1-893699-31-1

Librarians/Media Specialists:
PCIP/MARC records available **free of charge** at
www.americanchillers.com

Cover illustration by Dwayne Harris
Cover layout and design by Sue Harring

Copyright © 2011 AudioCraft Publishing, Inc. All rights reserved.
AMERICAN CHILLERS® , MICHIGAN CHILLERS® and
FREDDIE FERNORTNER, FEARLESS FIRST GRADER® are
registered trademarks of
AudioCraft Publishing, Inc.

Printed in USA

IDAHO
ICE
BEAST

VISIT CHILLERMANIA!

WORLD HEADQUARTERS FOR BOOKS BY JOHNATHAN RAND!

Yooperland

Indian River

Alpena

Traverse City

MICHIGAN

CHILLERMANIA!

*I-75 Exit 313
then south
1 mile!*

Mt. Pleasant

Bay City

Grand Rapids

Lansing

Detroit

Kalamazoo

Visit the HOME for books by Johnathan Rand! Featuring books, hats, shirts, bookmarks and other cool stuff not available anywhere else in the world! Plus, watch the American Chillers website for news of special events and signings at *CHILLERMANIA!* with author Johnathan Rand! Located in northern lower Michigan, on I-75! Take exit 313 . . . then south 1 mile! For more info, call (231) 238-0338. And be afraid! Be veeeery afraaaaaaiiiid . . . .

"Jessica, Mom says if you don't get out of bed right now, you're not going on the trip!"

Those words were spoken by my little brother, who had opened my bedroom door and was peeking inside.

"Get out of my room, Garrett," I said from beneath the covers.

I had no idea what time it was, but I was tired. Oh, I was excited about the trip and all that, but it was the reason I couldn't get to sleep the night before. Which, of course, was the reason I hadn't gotten out of bed when my alarm went off.

11

I just hit the snooze button and covered my head with my pillow. I was so tired, and all I wanted was a little more sleep.

But I knew it wasn't going to happen. We were headed to Sun Valley for a ski trip, and I knew I had to get up and get ready. Most of my things were already packed, so I didn't have much more to do.

And even though I was tired, I really was excited. Every winter, my family travels from our home in Boise, Idaho to Sun Valley, Idaho, where we stay at a lodge for a week. We ski, snowshoe, snowboard, ride inner tubes down hills . . . it's a week of great fun. I've always loved the winter, and I always look forward to our trip to Sun Valley.

But there's something else about Sun Valley that has always fascinated me:

Bigfoot. The Abominable Snowman. Yeti. Sasquatch. Or whatever you want to call it. Some people who've seen the creature around Sun Valley call it the Ice Beast.

Now, before you think I'm totally crazy, you need to know that I don't actually believe in the monster. But many people do, and I like to think that, somewhere in the mountains, maybe a bigfoot creature really does exist. After all, many people have claimed to have seen Bigfoot, and some people have even taken pictures. All of the pictures are either blurry or out of focus, so you never really get a good look at the beast. But it's fun to think about, and I often wonder if such a creature really does exist, hiding in the mountains somewhere.

I had no idea that I was about to get my answer, and I certainly had no idea that our fun vacation was going to turn into a terrifying experience that would change my life forever.

It took me a while, but I finally dragged myself out of bed and into the kitchen. I was so tired that I forgot to put on my slippers.

"I was just coming to get you," Mom said. "I thought you were going to sleep forever."

"I couldn't get to sleep last night," I replied with a yawn. "I kept thinking about our trip and how much fun we're going to have, even though I knew I needed to get to sleep. I'm so tired." I yawned again as I covered my mouth with my

15

hand.

"Well," Mom said, "maybe you can sleep in the car for a little while. It's a three hour drive to Sun Valley, but it will take us a little longer this time, because we're picking up your cousins."

That got me even more excited. Our cousins live in Mountain Home, which is another city in Idaho, south of Boise. To get to Sun Valley, we have to go through Mountain Home, and this year our cousins would be joining us on our vacation. My favorite cousin is Isaac. He's twelve years old, just like me. In fact, our birthdays are only a couple of weeks apart. He loves to do a lot of the same things that I do, and I knew we would have a great time at the resort in Sun Valley.

I wolfed down a bowl of cereal, got dressed, packed the rest of my things, and was finally ready to go. Dad, Mom, Garrett, and I piled into the car, and we were on our way by seven o'clock. Dad insisted that we get started early, so we could get to Sun Valley before noon. That way, he said, we'd have the rest of the day to ski.

I slept all the way to Mountain Home. Garrett brought a book with him, so he kept busy reading and didn't bug me. When we arrived at our cousins' house, they were ready to go. Isaac rode with us; the rest of his family followed us in their vehicle, and we drove the rest of the way to the resort at Sun Valley.

It was in the lobby of the resort where I first had an indication that our week-long trip wasn't going to be nearly as fun as I'd imagined.

Dad was at the front desk, getting checked in. We'd hauled all of our gear inside and placed it on a cart, so we wouldn't have to drag any of it up stairs or on an elevator. My mom and my aunt and uncle stood nearby, chatting.

"Hey," Isaac said as he picked up a newspaper from a coffee table by the fireplace. "Check this out!"

He held out the newspaper. On the front was a blurry, black and white photograph that appeared to show some sort of creature hiding among trees, boulders, and snow.

"*Is this the Idaho Ice Beast?*" I read the headline aloud.

"It looks like some sort of white bigfoot creature," Isaac said. "It says he was spotted not far from here."

"It's not real," I said. "There's no such thing."

Isaac shook his head. "Yes, there is," he said. "But he stays hidden in the mountains, so not many people see him. Wouldn't it be cool to see him during our vacation?"

"Sure," I said, "if he was real. But he's not real, and that picture is a fake."

I continued staring at the picture. Yes, it looked like some sort of creature was peering out between snow-covered pine trees, but it could have been just a trick of light and shadow. I didn't believe for a minute that it was actually some sort of creature.

Yet, something about the picture made me feel uneasy. I didn't believe it was a real creature, but the more I stared at it, the more anxious I became.

What if there really is some sort of weird creature out there? I thought. *What if he hunts people? What if his favorite snack is kids on snowshoes or skis?*

I can be that way, sometimes. Sometimes, I let my imagination run wild, and I get freaked out.

Well, I was going to get freaked out on our vacation, for sure . . . but it would have nothing to do with my imagination.

The rest of the day was a lot of fun. After we loaded everything into our room, we ate lunch with my cousins and my aunt and uncle in the restaurant at the resort. I sat with Isaac, and we talked and laughed the entire time. He really is pretty cool, and I wished he lived closer to our home in Boise, because we get to see each other only a couple of times a year.

After lunch, everyone went skiing, except for Isaac and me. I like snowboarding better than skiing, and so does Isaac, so that's what we did. I'm not very good at it, but it sure is a lot of fun.

And every so often, while sailing down the hill, I would stare off into the woods and think about the creepy picture from the newspaper. That got me thinking about all the other people who claimed to have seen a bigfoot creature, and I started to wonder again.

What if there really is a creature like that, living in the forest? What if he's watching me, right now.

But these thoughts vanished quickly. I had to pay attention to the hill, to what I was doing so I wouldn't crash into anything or anyone. Still, I fell a bunch of times, but I didn't get hurt. Actually, it was kind of fun.

That night, we had pizza in our room, which was connected to our cousins' room through a door. We all ate together. Then, Isaac, his little sister Sarah, my little brother Garrett, and I watched a movie. It was good, but I had a hard time keeping my eyes open. After all, I'd hardly slept the night before, so I got sleepy early, even though I'd napped for a little while on the way to Sun Valley. I changed into my pajamas and fell asleep on the couch . . . and that's where I was when I woke up some time during the night.

It was dark, and I was confused. There was a window with a curtain drawn, letting in a little light around the edges. It took me a moment to realize where I was.

Oh, yeah, I thought. *We're in Sun Valley, on our trip. I must have fallen asleep.*

The hotel room had two separate bedrooms: one for Garrett and me and one for my parents. I didn't want to sleep on the couch for the rest of the night, so I slowly stood and walked across the room. The door to Mom and Dad's room was open a tiny bit, and the door to my room was open all the way. There was a tiny nightlight glowing inside, and I could see the lumpy figure of Garrett sleeping beneath the covers on his bed.

I walked into the room. Like the larger living room, our bedroom also had a window. The curtains were closed, but thin bands of sugary light seemed to burn around the edges.

I wonder if it's snowing, I thought, and I tiptoed to the window and drew open the curtain.

Outside, several bright lights lit up the snow-covered parking area in the distance. We were on the third floor, so I had a good view of the ski hills, as they, too, had a few lights positioned up the mountain. The snow was falling lightly, and I was sure we would get a few inches by morning.

I was just about to let go of the curtain and allow it to fall back into place, when I saw something move. Something big, in the shadows near the trees.

I stopped and squinted, trying to see better. *Nothing.*

I continued watching, trying to see what had moved. I saw something, I was sure, but I didn't know what.

Finally, after not seeing it again, I climbed into bed and fell asleep.

The next morning, I awoke well rested,

excited, and ready for the day. I had completely forgotten about the thing I'd seen moving during the night . . . until Isaac and I went downstairs for breakfast.

That's when we saw a police car parked in front of the resort beneath the awning, and I was sure something horrible had happened.

When Isaac and I saw the uniformed man and woman in the lobby, we stopped.

"Uh-oh," Isaac whispered. *"Somebody's in trouble."*

It was then that I remembered seeing the strange sight outside the hotel room window last night, and I wondered if that had something to do with the police being there.

I knew I saw something, I thought. *There was something out there last night. Something in the shadows, near the trees.*

"Jessica?" Isaac said. "What's the matter? You look like you've seen a ghost."

"Not a ghost," I said. "But I saw something last night. Something in the snow, outside by the woods."

"What was it?" Isaac asked.

I shrugged. "I'm not really sure," I replied. "It was late, and it was dark. I saw something move, but I didn't really get a good look at what it was."

We started walking again, making our way past the two police officers at the front desk. I wanted to know why they were there, but I didn't want to be nosy. It really wasn't any of my business, but I still wondered if it had anything to do with the strange thing I had seen the night before.

Just what did I see? I wondered again. *I saw something move, I know that much. But I don't know what; it could've been a man, or maybe just a tree branch.*

The restaurant was connected to the lobby, and Isaac and I walked through a set of double doors. It was still a little early, so there weren't many people having breakfast yet. We chose a table that had enough chairs for everyone in my family and Isaac's, and then we sat.

Isaac turned his head and looked at the police officers.

"Maybe there was a robbery," Isaac said. "Or maybe there's a crazed killer on the loose!"

A woman came over to our table and smiled, filling up our water glasses.

"Can I get you two something for breakfast?" she asked.

"Not yet," I said. "We're waiting for our families to join us."

"How come the police are here?" Isaac asked her.

The server turned and looked at the two police officers standing by the front desk in the lobby.

"Oh, that," she said. "No big deal. Someone

29

drove their car into another car in the parking lot. It's slippery out there today. Nobody got hurt, but one of the cars has a big dent. Whenever that happens, they have to file a police report."

That made sense, and I was glad to hear that it had nothing to do with what I'd seen the night before. I was still a little nervous about the picture I'd seen in the paper the day before.

But I quickly forgot about bigfoot monsters when our families joined us for breakfast. We made plans for the day. Mom, Dad, and my aunt and uncle were going to ski. Garrett and my cousin Sarah were enrolled in a ski class, so they would be busy the entire day.

I had planned on snowboarding, but Isaac showed me something else.

"Look at this," he said, and he pulled a folded brochure from his pocket. It was colorful, and as he unfolded it, I could see that it was a trail map.

"These are snowshoe trails," he said. "Let's rent snowshoes and go for a hike through the hills.

We might even see that weird bigfoot creature that we saw in the newspaper yesterday."

I rolled my eyes. "Yeah, right," I said. "But snowshoeing sounds like it would be a lot of fun. Have you ever done it before?"

"Only once," Isaac replied. "It's great, once you get the hang of it. Snowshoes allow you to walk in snow that's really deep. You can even run while wearing them, but it takes some practice."

"Why would anyone want to run with snowshoes?" I asked.

Isaac shrugged. "Beats me," he said. "I'm not planning on running with my snowshoes on."

"Me, neither," I said.

But we were both wrong. Soon, both of us would be running with our snowshoes on . . . but we would be running to save our lives.

After breakfast we all returned to our rooms to get ready for the day. The warmest it was supposed to get was about thirty degrees. That's not all that cold, but we would still need to dress warmly. Especially Isaac and me. Everyone else in our families would be able to go into the lodge to get warm if they got cold on the slopes. But because we would be on the trails most of the day, there wouldn't be anyplace where we could go to get warm.

I put on my snow pants, coat, hat, and boots and then picked up my gloves. Everyone else was putting on their outdoor clothing, too.

Isaac came into the room. He, too, was wearing snow pants and a coat, and he had on a dorky-looking blue and yellow pointed hat with a fuzzy white dingle-ball on top. He pointed to it.

"Cool, huh?" he said.

"You look goofy," I replied.

Isaac grinned. "That's the point," he said. "Look what else I got."

He held out his hand and displayed a small leather bag.

"What's in it?" I asked.

"It's a survival kit," Isaac explained. He pulled the drawstring and emptied the contents on the counter. Items in the bag included a small package of bandages, a mini flashlight, a book of waterproof matches, a compass, a small spool of fishing line, a mirror, a whistle, a pocket knife, and a tiny sewing kit.

I picked up the small mirror. "What do you

use this for?" I asked.

"If you get lost," he said, "you can use it to signal for help by using the sun's reflection."

"What if it's a cloudy day?" I asked.

"Then, nobody finds you, and the bears eat you," Isaac replied with a playful smile.

That's Isaac for you. Always kidding around.

Dad gave me some money for my snowshoe rental and food. At the store on the first floor of the resort, we bought some wrapped sandwiches, a couple of apples, and candy bars. Then, we went to the rental place. Soon, Isaac and I were stepping outside, carrying our rented snowshoes. They were big—about three times the size of my boots—and made of aluminum with rawhide lacings that crisscrossed back and forth. Each snowshoe had a harness to strap on a boot so it wouldn't fall off while you walked.

"I don't see how these are going to keep our feet from sinking into the snow," I said as we put our snowshoes on the ground and laced them to our boots.

"They really do," Isaac said. "You'll see."

He was right. It took a minute to get used to walking with the snowshoes strapped to my boots, but I got the hang of it. It was actually a lot of fun. When we left the ski area and went into spots where the snow was deep, we sank only a few inches.

"The snow is about two feet deep here," Isaac said. "If we didn't have snowshoes, we would sink and it would be impossible to walk. Ready to head for the trail?"

"In a minute," I replied. "I want to check on something. Follow me."

"Where?" Isaac asked, but I didn't reply. Instead, I headed through the deep snow on my snowshoes, making my way to the place where I'd seen the movement the night before.

I'm sure it was nothing, I thought, but I still wanted to make sure. There was no harm in looking, was there?

Was there?

I poked around the trees and looked for

signs of disturbed snow.

Sure enough, there were footprints in the fresh powder that had fallen overnight.

Enormous footprints that were much bigger than any human could make.

If we had been smart, we would have left them alone or maybe told someone at the resort.

But we were curious . . . and sometimes, curiosity can get you into big trouble, as we were about to find out.

"That's totally freaky," Isaac said as we looked at the tracks in the snow. They were big—almost as big as the tracks made by our snowshoes—and they circled around a couple of trees before leading off into the woods.

"I knew I saw something last night," I said.

"Do you think it was a man?" Isaac asked.

"Why would someone be out in the middle of the night?" I said, and I pointed to the tracks that led off into the forest. "And why would

39

someone go out into the woods at night like that?"

"Maybe it was the creature we saw in the paper!" Isaac said.

"I don't know," I replied, shaking my head. "It was dark, and I didn't get a good look at it."

We stood in silence for a moment, our breath fogging in the cold, winter air.

Finally, I spoke. "Let's follow the tracks and see where they lead. There must be an explanation, because there's no such thing as abominable snowmen, bigfoot creatures, or ice beasts."

"Okay," Isaac said. "And if we get lost, I've got my emergency survival kit."

"And I have a phone," I said. "If something goes wrong, we can call for help. The phone has a camera, too, so if we *do* see anything unusual, I can take a picture."

We started out. I was a little clumsy on the snowshoes, and I fell a couple of times, but the snow was deep and soft, and I didn't get hurt. Isaac fell once or twice, too.

But soon, we both got the hang of having the large contraptions attached to our feet. It was actually kind of cool, being able to walk across deep snow like that, without sinking down to our waists.

"See anything?" I asked. We hadn't gone very far, and I really hadn't expected to come across anyone or anything. After all, if the tracks had been made last night, whatever made them could be miles away by now, and then we'd never know what had made them.

"Nope," Isaac said. "But I'm having fun with these snowshoes."

I was puzzled. I refused to believe that some strange creature had made the tracks, but I thought they looked much bigger than what an adult would make. Besides: the snow was deep. Any adult would probably get tired walking in that much snow without the aid of snowshoes.

So, what created these big footprints? I wondered as we continued to follow the deep tracks through the woods.

I kept watching, looking for signs of anything, totally unaware that a creature was watching Isaac and me at that very moment, hiding unseen beneath the tightly-knotted limbs of a spruce tree.

Finally, when I was only a few feet away, the beast made his move. It lunged out with such speed and power that I knew for certain there was no way I would be able to outrun it . . . and with snowshoes strapped to each foot, there wasn't a single thing I could do.

7

Isaac was just as frightened as I was. The noise and sudden motion were really close and had taken us completely by surprise. Isaac shrieked, and I fell, but not before I got a glimpse of the huge mule deer that had been hiding beneath the web of tangled branches and limbs. He'd been there all along, probably hoping that we didn't get too close. When we did, he got scared and took off. His sudden bolt from his hiding place scared the daylights out of Isaac and me.

We watched as the big deer thundered off through the forest. He didn't seem to have any trouble at all with the deep snow.

I stood, but it was a bit challenging with the snowshoes strapped to my boots.

"That thing scared the heck out of me!" Isaac said. "I thought it was the ice beast attacking!"

"He freaked me out, too," I said, and I looked around to see if there might be more deer hiding among the trees and branches. I didn't see any, and I was glad. I didn't want to be surprised like that again.

"Want to keep going?" I asked.

"Sure," Isaac said. "It's not like we can get lost, because we can always follow our tracks back to the resort."

"It's kind of fun exploring on our own," I said. "We get to see things that other people would miss."

"Like a giant, killer deer," Isaac smirked.

We started out again, and I kept my eyes

open for anything that might surprise us. In Idaho, there are all kinds of animals to see, all year. In the summer, my dad loves to fly fish, and he says he sees a lot of black bears when he goes into the wilderness. He even carries a bell with him that makes noise when he walks, so he doesn't accidentally sneak up and surprise a bear. He says that if the bear hears him coming, he'll go away. Dad says the last thing you want to do is surprise a bear.

But it was winter, and most black bears hibernate in dens during the cold weather, so I was pretty sure we didn't have anything to worry about. Oh, there are a few grizzly bears in Idaho, but not very many. I've never seen any, except in a zoo. I wasn't worried about coming across a bear, but there was a good chance we might see another mule deer, and I didn't want to go through another scare like the one we'd already had.

I pressed on, following the tracks as they wound through the snow, constantly wondering what kind of creature could have made them.

"You know," I said as I trudged along on my snowshoes, "we'll probably find out that the tracks were made by someone with big boots. What do you think?"

Isaac didn't answer.

I turned. "Isaac—"

He wasn't there. Isaac had been walking behind me just a moment before . . . but now, he was gone!

"Isaac?" I called out. My voice echoed through the cold, snowy forest, then died out.

"Quit playing around," I called out. "You're hiding from me, and I know it."

"Rats!" came his voice from somewhere in the forest. Then, he appeared from behind a large tree trunk. "I was hoping you'd think I was eaten by the ice beast."

"Fat chance of that," I said. "Your goofy hat would probably scare him away."

Isaac plodded toward me on his snowshoes.

"You know," he said, "these could really come in handy. I'd like to have a pair of these at home. I could walk all over the place."

"It is a lot of fun," I agreed.

We continued following the tracks through the woods, over small hills and around large chunks of gigantic gray boulders and rock formations that protruded from the ground. Finally, we stopped at the top of a small hill and gazed around. The new snow on the tree branches was beautiful, and a fine, powdery snow was falling from the ashen sky.

"How far do you think we've gone?" Isaac asked.

"We haven't been out for very long," I replied. "I don't think we've gone more than a mile. Do you want to turn around?"

Isaac took off his gloves and dug into his coat pocket. He pulled out the trail map and unfolded it.

"You really do look like a dork with that hat

on," I said, pointing at his head. "I'm glad no one else is around. I'd be embarrassed to be seen with you."

Isaac just grinned and studied the map.

"I think," he said as he drew an imaginary line on the map with a finger, "that if we keep going, we'll come across one of these hiking trails. So, we might as well keep following the tracks, as long as they don't make any weird turns." Then, he returned the map to his pocket.

"Fine with me," I said. I knew we wouldn't get lost because we could easily backtrack.

But there was one thing I hadn't counted on.

The weather.

It had been snowing lightly, but suddenly the flakes became huge. They were the size of cotton balls, and they fell thick and heavy. Actually, it was kind of cool looking, because it was snowing so hard that it was difficult to see very far.

And we still hadn't found a single trail, and we hadn't come across any other person. In fact, it looked as if the forest was getting thicker and thicker.

We stopped. Isaac looked even sillier, now that his cone-shaped hat had a mantle of snow covering it. He pulled out his map once again.

"I don't understand," he said. "We should have come to a trail by now."

"Well," I said, "I don't think we're going to find whatever it is that made these tracks. We should head back."

"Okay," Isaac said reluctantly. He again returned the map to his coat pocket, and we turned around to follow our tracks back to the resort.

And that's where our trouble first began. It was snowing so hard, and the flakes were so big, that the snow was quickly covering over our tracks. Even the bigger, deeper tracks that we had been following were filling in. Soon, the tracks vanished completely. We had to stop walking, because we weren't sure in which direction to head. There were no sounds, nothing to give us any indication of which way to go.

This isn't good, I thought with growing concern. *This isn't good at all.*

We were in the middle of a snowstorm in the foothills around Sun Valley . . . and we were lost.

"I think we should go that way," Isaac said, raising his hand and pointing. "I have a gut feeling about these things."

"I do, too," I replied. I pointed in the opposite direction. "But I think we should go *that* way."

The snow continued to fall. I couldn't believe how heavy and thick it was. There were no signs of our previous tracks at all. It was as if we hadn't even been trudging through the snow.

"Well, we're not far from the resort," Isaac said. "We should be able to find it easy enough."

I shook my head. "Don't count on it," I said. "Maybe the best thing to do is just to wait here for a while to see if the snow lets up. Then, we can look for our tracks. Maybe the snow hasn't covered all of them. But right now, it's snowing so hard that I can hardly see the trees."

Isaac unzipped his coat and dug into an inside pocket. He pulled out his emergency survival kit. Then, he took off his gloves, opened the drawstring on the kit, and fumbled around inside the small bag. Finally, he pulled out the compass.

"Unfortunately, this isn't going to do us any good," he said. "We didn't pay attention to which direction we were heading when we left the resort. We have no idea if we should head north, south, east, or west." So, Isaac put the compass back in the bag.

"If we *are* lost," I said, "and my parents have to come looking for us, I am going to be in a lot of trouble."

"You and me both," Isaac said. "My parents will take away my video games for weeks."

"My parents will ground me from the library for a month," I said. "I go there a couple of days every week to get books. If I can't go to the library, I don't know what I'm going to do."

"Right now, instead of thinking about the trouble we're *going* to be in, let's think about the trouble we *are* in. We're lost, sort of. But let's just stay calm and cool and figure a way out of this."

So, that's what we did. We stayed right where we were, standing on our snowshoes, watching the snow falling all around us. It showed no signs of letting up. However, we were sure we'd be okay. We weren't worried about being lost as much as we were worried about getting into trouble when we were found.

In fact, we were so wrapped up in thinking about being lost in the heavy snow that we had completely forgotten about the reason we were in the woods in the first place. We'd forgotten that we had been following tracks in the snow. Tracks that we didn't think belonged to a human being.

And while we stood there with the giant snowflakes falling all around, piling up on tree branches and on the ground, covering any and all of the tracks we had made, we had no idea that the creature that had made those tracks had been following us, and at that very moment, was watching us, waiting . . . .

The snow continued to fall.

"Well," Isaac said hopefully, "at least we have my emergency survival kit. We can build a fire if we need to, so we won't freeze."

"And we have a little bit of food," I said, "so we won't starve."

"Now that you mention it," Isaac said, "I *am* a little bit hungry." He dug into his pocket and pulled out a candy bar. "I think I'm going to have a little snack."

I was kind of hungry, too, so I pulled out the apple I had bought and bit into it. It was juicy and sweet.

While I ate, I looked around. The heavy snowflakes created a really beautiful scene. I know some people don't like winter because it can be so cold, but I love it. I love the snow and being outdoors. I love skiing and snowboarding and riding inner tubes down hills. And now I had a new hobby: snowshoeing.

Next time, I thought, *I think it would be best to stay on a trail.*

Isaac spoke. "When we get back, I'm going to—"

His words were stopped short by a strange, growling sound. It was long and mournful, and I'd never heard anything like it.

We stopped eating and listened. I was toasty and warm all bundled up in my winter clothing, but the sound sent a cold shiver through my body.

"Did . . . did you . . . did you hear that?" Isaac stammered.

"Shhhh," I replied. *"Listen."*

We listened, but we didn't hear anything. The snow fell silently, and there wasn't even any wind to cause the tree branches to tremble.

Slowly, Isaac took another bite of his candy bar. We continued to search the forest around us for any sign of movement. We saw nothing but the wall of thick snowflakes.

"That sure sounded weird," Isaac said. "What do you think it was?"

"I have no idea," I replied. I turned my head slowly, straining to see through the densely falling snow. All I could think about was the photograph I'd seen in the newspaper the day before. The headline ran through my mind.

Is this the Idaho Ice Beast?

No. There is no such thing.

I raised the apple to my mouth and was about to take another bite, when the sound came again. Was it my imagination, or did it sound even closer? And from which direction was it coming? The strange growling snarl echoed through the forest, and it seemed to come from all directions, all around us. The sound was inhuman.

When it faded away, I suddenly realized I was shaking, and it had nothing to do with the cold weather.

Isaac was shaking, too. "Do you think it's the creature we saw in the newspaper?" he asked. "The Idaho Ice Beast?"

"I was just thinking the same thing," I said quietly. While I spoke, I continued to scan the forest. "But it's not possible. Creatures like that don't exist."

"I sure hope you're right," Isaac said. "I wouldn't want to be lost in the forest with one of those things running loose."

Then, we heard another sound. A branch snapping. A rustling sound. Isaac and I turned to see a thick lump of snow falling from a tree branch.

But it was the gigantic creature beneath the limb that got our attention.

I had never believed in Bigfoot, or the ice

beast, or whatever you wanted to call him. I thought the creature was just a myth, and all of the pictures were phony. Not once had I ever thought that such an animal could or would exist. Not in Idaho, not anywhere.

And yet, here I was, faced with the fact that I was staring at the same creature I'd seen in the newspaper the day before. He just stood there, a massive, muscular beast that stood upright, covered with hair and snow, watching us watching him.

Then, he took a step toward us. And another. Still another.

He stopped. His head cocked to the side, as if he sensed something. He sniffed the air.

Suddenly, he let out another horrible growling snarl . . . and came at us.

I think what made our situation even worse was the fact that we were lost in the woods and had no idea where to run. On top of that, we both had snowshoes strapped to our boots. While it would be almost impossible to move through the deep snow without the snowshoes, they still made our movements much slower than normal.

The attacking creature, however, seemed to have no difficulty moving through the snow at all. He was several feet taller than a normal human being, and his legs were big and strong. He trudged through the snow as easily as the mule deer we'd seen.

There were two things that spared us from falling into the clutches of the gigantic creature. First of all, although the creature moved through the snow with ease, he wasn't moving very fast. It seemed to me that if he really was determined to come after us, he would have moved faster.

Still, when the beast started heading in our direction, Isaac and I didn't waste any time. We turned and began to run—as best we could on our snowshoes—in the opposite direction.

The second thing that helped us escape was when Isaac dropped his candy bar. I don't know if he even realized it at the time. Neither one of us gave any thought to anything, except getting away from the attacking beast.

However, the candy bar saved us, at least for the time being. When the creature approached the candy bar in the snow, he stopped. Then, he knelt down, sniffed the morsel, picked it up in his claw, and ate it . . . wrapper and all!

This gave us some time to get away. We trudged on as fast as we could on our snowshoes. Soon, we couldn't see the creature through the trees or the densely falling snow.

When we finally stopped, we were out of breath, and our lungs were heaving. The cold air chilled my throat.

"We have to keep moving," I said, between gasps.

"But where are we going to go?" Isaac asked. "We have no idea where we are or which direction we should head in."

"It doesn't matter," I said. "Sooner or later, that thing is going to come after us again. We need to get as far away from it as we can."

"Why don't we take our snowshoes off and climb a tree?" Isaac suggested.

I thought about this for a moment, but I decided against it.

"No," I said, "that won't work. What if the creature can climb trees? Or what if he's strong enough to knock the tree over? If we climb a tree, we'll be stuck. Plus, if we don't have our snowshoes on, we'll never be able to make it through this heavy snow."

So, we pressed on as fast as we could. We tried to run, and I think we succeeded a little bit. Actually, it was more like a clumsy jog. But we were able to move faster than simply walking, and we were certainly moving faster than we would if we didn't have the snowshoes on.

The good news was that every time I looked over my shoulder—which was often—I saw no sign of the ice beast coming after us. I don't know if he had actually attacked us, or perhaps he had smelled the candy bar. Maybe that's what he wanted all along.

No matter. The beast was gigantic, and he looked hideous. I was certain that he would continue to come after us.

That was another thing: Isaac and I still had food in our coats. What if the ice beast could smell our sandwiches? What if he could smell the half-eaten apple that I had quickly tucked into my pocket when we began running away from the beast?

"Hey, Isaac," I began. "Maybe we should—"

I was interrupted by Isaac's sudden shriek.

"Hey!" he shouted, raising his arm and pointing with his glove. "Look!"

I couldn't believe our luck. Ahead of us, tucked beneath some trees, was a small cabin! It looked dark, and I didn't think anyone was home. But maybe we could get inside! If we could, we would be safe.

"Let's go!" I said excitedly, and we trudged over the snow in our snowshoes faster than ever. In less than a minute, we had reached the cabin, where we quickly discovered that the front door was unlocked. Isaac and I hurried inside, slammed the door shut, and then found a deadbolt lock. I slid it closed, and it anchored with a loud thunking sound.

We had made it. We were safe.

But not for long.

It was gloomy and dim inside the cabin, which was constructed of dark, hand-hewn logs. The only light came from a single window that had a closed curtain. In the twilight-like atmosphere, I could see that there were only two additional rooms: a small bedroom and a bathroom. In fact, my bedroom was only a little bit smaller than the entire cabin. The main room where we stood was not only a kitchen, but a dining room and the living room. There was a refrigerator next to some cupboards, a dining table with two chairs, and an old recliner. A television sat on an ancient desk against the far wall. Like I said: the cabin was tiny.

"Now what?" Isaac said.

"I'm going to call my dad," I said.

I dug into my coat pocket and pulled out my phone. I tried to dial out, but the call wouldn't go through.

"Come on," I said as I pressed the speed dial number again. "Come on."

"What's the matter?" Isaac asked.

"I don't have a signal," I answered. "We must be too far away from any cell towers." I pocketed my phone. "Well, so much for that."

"Great," Isaac said. "We're being chased by a killer ice beast, and no one knows what's going on. Nobody knows where we are. Even *we* don't know where we are."

"We've got to think," I said. "We're safe for the time being. Let's put our heads together and figure out what to do. I'm just glad we found this cabin, and I'm even more glad the door was unlocked."

"I hope the owners don't come back to find us here," Isaac said. "We'll get into a lot of trouble and probably get arrested. We'll probably go to jail until we're ninety years old."

"By the looks of it," I said, "this appears to be a summer cabin. Otherwise, we would have seen a driveway. It doesn't look like anyone has been here for a while."

To prove my point, I walked to the refrigerator. Not only was it empty, but it wasn't even plugged in.

"See?" I said as I held up the unplugged black cord. "No one is living here. It's not like we broke in, and we're certainly not going to take anything. We just needed a safe place to get away from the ice beast. I don't think we'll get into trouble or be arrested for that."

Isaac walked to the window and drew back the curtain. He looked outside and flinched.

"We've got trouble!" he said as he turned his head toward me. Then, he looked out the window again. "That ugly thing followed us!"

I hurried over to the window and looked outside. Sure enough, the ice beast was making his way through the snowy forest, following our tracks that led to the cabin.

To our hiding place.

"I hope he doesn't know we're hiding in here," Isaac said.

"We'll know in a minute," I said. "I don't know if he can smell us or if he's following our tracks. But he's coming our way."

We watched the horrific ice beast as he came closer and closer to the cabin. Then, we couldn't see him any more, as he was on the other side of the structure and out of our line of sight.

"He's almost here," Isaac breathed.

Then, we heard sounds. Breaking branches. Shuffling. Crunching snow.

Then, there was a scratch at the door that made my skin crawl. It sounded like a fingernail on a blackboard. We could hear the creature breathing slowly and heavily. In and out.

In and out . . . .

"Isaac," I whispered. *"I don't like the sound of this. I don't like the sound of this at all."*

The ice beast was inches away from the cabin door. The question was: could he—or would he—break down the door to get us?

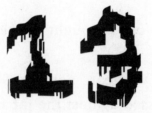

13

Tense seconds ticked past. We could hear the beast on the other side of the door, breathing. In my mind, I could see his nostrils flaring, and I could imagine his frosty breath in the cold winter air.

Isaac and I had slowly walked backward in the cabin to get as far away from the front door as we could. Now, our backs were pressed against the wall, and we were motionless, waiting for the door to come crashing down, waiting for the horrific beast to come storming in.

There was more scratching on the door. Every scrape made my muscles tense. I don't think I've ever been so frightened in my life.

Then, we heard more shuffling sounds, and the sound of snow being crushed. The sound slowly faded.

Could it be? I thought. *Is the monster going away?*

Finally, we heard nothing. Still, Isaac and I remained pressed against the far wall, silent and listening.

"Do you think he's gone?" Isaac whispered.

"I think so," I replied quietly.

We relaxed a little. Although we might still be in danger, the ice beast hadn't smashed down the door and attacked us like I thought he would.

I pulled out my phone again and looked for any sign of a signal. There was none. Just in case, however, I tried dialing Dad again. Again, the call didn't go through.

"Now what?" Isaac said.

"I don't know," I said. "But I'm sure glad we

found this cabin. I can't imagine what would've happened to us if we hadn't come across it."

"We would have been monster food," Isaac said. "Which would've been too bad. I don't taste very good without salt."

I laughed out loud. Even in the serious situation we were in and the very real danger that confronted us, Isaac still had a sense of humor.

"Maybe he carries around his own salt shaker," I said.

"Maybe he'd take us back to his cave and grill us," Isaac snickered.

Again, I laughed, and it felt good. Maybe we were going to get out of this alive, after all.

But at that moment, an enormous shadow fell over the window . . . and I realized that our ordeal wasn't over. It was only just beginning.

We didn't dare move.

"*He's back!*" Isaac hissed.

"*Shhh!*" I whispered back. "*He might not know we're in here.*"

The shadow over the window moved, but we had no idea how close he was to the cabin, because the curtains were closed. We knew he was there, though, because the light around the edge of the curtains dimmed.

I wish my phone worked, I thought. *I wish we*

would've stayed on the trail and not followed those tracks. Then, we wouldn't be in this mess.

Once again, we could hear the creature breathing.

"He knows we're here, all right," Isaac whispered. *"He knows we're inside, and he's going to come and get us."*

"Be quiet!" I hissed.

The shadow moved away from the window, but we could hear the beast creeping along the outside wall of the cabin as he crunched through the snow. He went all around the small building, circling us like a wolf circling its prey. Once again, he stopped at the front door. The doorknob jangled, and we heard a few scratches.

Both Isaac and I tensed, waiting for the door to break open, waiting to see the enormous form of the hideous beast in the doorway, knowing there was nowhere for us to run.

Once again, I realized how vulnerable we were. While I was glad we had found the cabin, I still wasn't sure if it would keep the ice beast from getting to us. If he was strong enough to break down the door, the cabin might just become our tomb.

But when the creature once again moved away, we heaved huge sighs of relief. We waited for several minutes to make sure the beast was gone before we spoke.

"We have to figure out what we're going to do," I said quietly. "We can't stay here forever, but it's not safe to leave the cabin."

"Are you sure your phone won't work?" Isaac asked.

I pulled out my phone and looked at it.

"No bars," I said, shaking my head. "I can't even send a text message."

"So, what are our options?" Isaac asked.

"Maybe this cabin has a phone," I said. "Let's look for it. Being that it is in the middle of the woods, I doubt it, but we have to try everything."

It didn't take us long to search the cabin and discover that I was right. There was no phone.

"Sooner or later," Isaac said, "our families

are going to realize we're missing. Someone is going to come looking for us."

"But we have no idea where we are," I replied. "And with the new snow, all of our tracks will be erased. We might have to plan on staying here for a couple of days."

"A couple of days!?!?" Isaac said. "Our food won't last that long! We'll starve to death!"

I glared at him and spoke. "What would you rather do: starve to death or be eaten by that creature that's after us?"

He thought about this.

"I think the best thing we can do is wait for a little while and then try to find a way back to the resort."

"That sounds like a great plan," I said, "but you and I both know we have no idea where the resort is. We might be in a cabin in the woods, but the fact of the matter is, we're lost. We're lost, and there is a gigantic ice beast out there, somewhere, and I have a feeling he's not going to go away."

I had just finished my sentence, and Isaac

was about to respond when the window exploded. Glass showered the tiny room, and the curtains were ripped open.

If we thought things were bad before, they had just gotten worse.

A lot worse.

Instead of running outside through the front door, we ran into the bedroom. It was something we did without thinking, as there was no way I was leaving the safety of the cabin. Sure, we didn't know how safe the cabin was . . . but I was certain that if we went outside, we would stand no chance at all.

I was first into the bedroom, followed by Isaac. He slammed the door.

"There's no lock!" he shrieked.

Frantically, I looked around the room. On the other side of the bed was a chair. I ran to it and brought it to the door, where I tilted it backward and propped the back beneath the doorknob.

"I don't know if that will hold," I said. "But it's better than nothing."

We could hear the beast snarling and growling, but it sounded like he was still outside.

"I don't think he can make it through the window," I said. "He's too big."

Isaac pointed. "But there's a window in here, too," he said. "What if he tries to get in this one?"

I turned to look at the window that Isaac was pointing at.

"That window is even smaller than the one in the living room," I said. "He might smash the glass, but I don't think there's any way he can get inside."

"But we have no idea how strong he is," Isaac said. "He might be able to smash the walls down."

Isaac had a point. The beast appeared to be incredibly muscular and was probably stronger than a horse. Our lives depended on the cabin being stronger than the creature.

There really wasn't anything we could do but wait. It was maddening. The feeling of helplessness combined with complete horror was overwhelming. I've never been in a situation where there was nothing I could do to help myself. Worse, there was no one who could help us, no one to come and save the day.

Gradually, over the course of a minute or two, silence returned. It didn't sound like the ice beast was banging around the window in the living room. I kept looking at the bedroom window, waiting for it to be smashed in, too.

"It wouldn't be so bad if we could see him," Isaac said. "If we knew what he was doing or where he was going, I would feel a lot better."

"We don't have any choice in the matter," I said. "We're like two mice backed into a corner by a cat. It's his game, and he's going to do what he wants."

Once again, we heard footsteps around the cabin as the creature walked around. There was no doubt he was trying to figure out how he could get inside and get at us.

Things got quiet once again . . . but not for long. There was a sudden, splintering explosion that shook the entire cabin, followed by a tremendous roar from the beast. The sound was so loud that we knew, without question, the creature was now inside the cabin. He had broken down the front door with little or no trouble at all.

And if he could break down the front door, I knew he would be able to easily smash in the bedroom door.

We were sitting ducks.

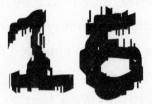

Isaac opened his mouth to speak, but I quickly placed my gloved hand over his mouth.

"Shhhh," I whispered. *"Be quiet."*

"He has to know we're in here!" Isaac hissed.

"Maybe not," I said quietly. *"Remember: he's an animal. He's not human. He's probably not as intelligent as us."*

"Yeah," Isaac agreed, *"but he probably has a lot better sense of smell than we do. We probably smell like juicy hamburgers, and our scent will lead*

him right to us in this bedroom."

I hated to admit it, but Isaac was probably right. I wasn't sure how smart the creature was, but he probably had an excellent sense of smell and very good eyesight.

On the other side of the bedroom door, we could hear the beast rummaging around the living room. I heard a crash that sounded like the kitchen table being turned over.

"Maybe it's our food that he's after," Isaac said.

"You're right!" I whispered to Isaac. *"Maybe he smells the food in our coats! Maybe that's what he's after!"*

"Let's get rid of it!" said Isaac.

"Yeah," I said, with a nod. "But we have to be smart about it. If he's after our food, we have to use it to help us get away."

"What do you mean?" Isaac asked.

In the other room, we could hear the creature pawing around the kitchen. There were several crashes that sounded like ceramic dishes breaking on the floor.

I pointed to the bedroom window. "That window isn't big enough for the creature to go through," I said. "But we can."

I ran around the bed and drew back the curtain.

"This window slides open!" I hissed. I grabbed the window latch, slid it back, and pushed open the window. There was just enough room for us to squeeze through, but we would have to go one at a time.

"Quick!" I whispered as I unzipped my coat. My wrapped sandwich was tucked in an inside pocket, and I pulled it out and tossed it onto the bed. My half-eaten apple was in my left pocket, and I tossed it next to my sandwich. Isaac had pulled out his sandwich, along with the remaining candy bar, and dropped them next to my food on the bed.

"That might buy us some time," I said. "Let's crawl out the window and get out of here!"

Without warning, the door exploded into

pieces. It wasn't just knocked off its hinges . . . it was turned into kindling. The chair, too, suffered the same fate.

And standing in the doorway, not ten feet from where we stood, was the hideous ice beast.

"Get out the window!" I shouted, and I bounded onto the bed and leapt. I almost succeeded in diving out completely, but my legs hit the sill, and I dangled for a moment, half in and half out the window. Isaac, however, was right behind me. He grabbed my ankles and pushed, sending me tumbling outside, landing face first in the deep snow. I struggled for a moment before getting to my feet.

"Jessica!" Isaac screamed. "Help me! *Pull!*"

His hat had fallen off, and he was hanging halfway out the window. I grabbed his arms and pulled. He came down on top of me, and I fell back down into the deep snow.

Inside the cabin, the ice beast let out an ear-piercing wail, a deep, raging growl, vicious and angry. I hoped that he would find the food and be distracted away from us. It probably wouldn't take him very long to eat the sandwiches, apple, and the candy bar, but I wanted to get as far away as possible during that time.

Isaac stood, brushed the snow off his snow pants and coat, and helped me up.

"Let's get out of here!" I said.

But that's where we discovered another problem. We'd taken off our snowshoes by the front door of the cabin . . . and that's where they remained. Without them, we were forced to wade through waist-deep snow. It was maddeningly slow, tedious, and tiring. Every step seemed to engage every muscle in my legs and feet. It was like trying to move in deep mud.

"This isn't going to work," Isaac said in despair, and he stopped near an ancient tree stump. He was out of breath, and I was, too. "We're going to tire out real fast."

Isaac was right. We weren't going to be able to go very far without our snowshoes.

But what really scared me? The ice beast didn't seem to have any trouble at all moving through the snow. If he came at us now, there was no way we would get away. We would be helpless, powerless to do anything.

The snow continued to fall in big, cotton ball-size flakes. It looked like several inches had accumulated in just a short time. New snow coated the branches of the trees, making the limbs bend beneath the weight.

I turned around. We had gone only about fifty feet from the cabin. Our footsteps left gaping holes in the new snow, but the holes already seemed to be filling up with newly fallen flakes.

"My hat," Isaac said as he reached up and brushed snow from his hair. "I left it by the cabin."

"Don't go back for it now," I said.

"Rats," he said. "I really liked that hat."

And then I saw something I really didn't want to see.

The ice beast.

He was outside the cabin with his back toward us, looking in the opposite direction.

"Isaac," I said quietly. *"Don't move an inch. The ice beast is outside, but he's looking the other way. If we don't move, he might not see us."*

The ice beast turned. He sniffed the air. Once again, I was horrified at his monstrous size.

He looks like a great white ape that lifts weights, I thought. *The abominable snowman is a bodybuilder.*

"Don't move," I repeated quietly.

The ice beast was now looking directly at us.

Could he see us?

He tilted his head back and sniffed the air. Then, his head lowered and his gaze returned to us.

"This isn't looking good," Isaac whispered.

Slowly, the ice beast cocked his head to the side.

Then, to my horror, he began walking toward us through the deep snow, trudging easily with his powerful, muscular legs.

We had been spotted. We had been spotted, and without our snowshoes, we simply had no hope of escape.

Thirty seconds.

That's about how long I estimated it would take for the creature to reach us. It wasn't a lot of time for us to get away, and we certainly wouldn't be able to outrun the beast.

I snapped my head around.

"That tree!" I said, pointing. "It has some lower branches. Let's climb up it!"

"But you said that wasn't a good idea!" Isaac shouted.

"We don't have any choice!" I said. "Hurry up!"

I wasn't sure what kind of tree it was. Maybe an oak or maple. I couldn't tell, because there were no leaves on the branches. The only thing that mattered was that it was close by, and it had low branches that would allow us to climb up.

Isaac reached the tree first, and he began pulling himself up through the branches. I quickly followed. We scrambled up as fast as we could. It was harder than I thought. With my snow pants, gloves, coat, and boots, climbing was difficult and clumsy.

I tried not to look down very often to see how close the ice beast was, because every time I did, it took my attention away from my climb. Still, Isaac and I managed to make our way well up into the branches before the creature reached the tree. When I looked down, the ice beast was standing by the trunk, looking up curiously. It was as if he didn't know how we had gotten up into the tree.

"I don't think he can climb," Isaac said.

"I hope you're right," I said. "We might have to stay up here all day, just to be safe."

"I hope not," Isaac said.

"Me, too," I replied, "but if that's what we have to do, we don't have a choice in the matter."

Beneath us, the ice beast was circling the trunk, looking up. Without a doubt, he was trying to figure out a way to get us. I wondered if he even knew how to climb a tree. Maybe he was too big and bulky, or maybe he had just never done it before.

Regardless, I was glad. We had outwitted him again, at least for the time being.

The heavy snow continued to fall. It was building up on my arms and shoulders, and I carefully brushed it off while I held tightly to the tree branch I was clinging to.

"Uh-oh," Isaac said. "I think we spoke too soon."

I looked down. The ice beast had raised his arms and grasped one of the lower branches. While we watched, he pulled himself off the

101

ground, placing one of his enormous legs on a limb. Then, he reached for a higher branch and continued to pull.

He was climbing up, and there was nowhere for us to go.

The beast knew how to climb after all, or he was learning quickly.

Now we were *really* stuck. We were already so high that if we tried to go any farther up, the branches would bend and sway under our weight.

But if we had one thing going for us, it was the fact that the ice beast was a very slow climber. His size and bulk worked against him, and he seemed unsure and uncertain of his movements as he pulled himself up into the tree.

"Now, we're really in trouble," Isaac said. "What now?"

"I don't know," I replied. But that wasn't the truth. The truth was I had one last-ditch effort planned. I didn't want to do it; in fact, I didn't even want to tell Isaac about it. But if I had no other choice, I would.

I would jump.

Oh, I most likely wouldn't survive the fall. I would probably break every bone in my body. But even *that* seemed better than what the horrible ice beast would do to me.

Below us, the ice beast continued his slow climb. He was now only about twenty feet below us.

Isaac had been thinking the same thing.

"I'm going to jump!" he shouted. "I'm going to jump, because I'm not going to let that thing get me!"

"I am, too!" I shouted. "I'd rather jump than be eaten by that thing!"

Below us, the ice beast let out a loud snarl.

It was almost as if he was listening to us, as if he understood what we were saying.

But he continued to climb.

"Okay," I said. "Let's jump. On the count of three."

"Okay," Isaac said.

"One," I said.

The ice beast let out a roar.

"Two . . . ."

The ice beast kept coming. He was only two branches beneath me.

I closed my eyes. *It's over,* I thought. *My life is really over. But I am not going to let that thing get me.*

"Three!"

I was just about to let go of the branch I was
clinging to when I heard a loud snap below me.
Isaac was also just about ready to leap, but when
he heard the noise, he quickly wrapped his arm
around the branch before falling.

Beneath us, one of the branches had broken
under the heavy weight of the ice beast. He let out
a horrible roar as he fell. Branches bent and broke,
and he landed near the trunk, on his back, in the
deep snow.

Isaac and I said nothing. We stared down through the tree limbs, looking at the motionless creature.

Finally, Isaac spoke.

"Is he . . . is he dead?" he asked

"I don't know," I replied. "I hope so. If he's not dead, he's going to be even madder than he was before."

We continued watching the ice beast, looking for any signs of life: some movement or even a fine, frosty breath in the cold air. We saw nothing to indicate the creature was alive.

"I think he's dead," Isaac said. "I think the fall killed him."

While I was hopeful, I was still reluctant to climb down the tree. Even if the ice beast was dead, I didn't want to be anywhere near him.

"Let's wait for a few minutes," I said. "Just to be sure."

The seconds ticked by. Isaac and I were silent, and we kept our eyes on the motionless creature in the snow below us. The snow continued to fall, and very quickly, a thin layer of it had covered the creature.

"I think it's safe to go down," Isaac said. "Come on. Let's climb down, get our snowshoes, and figure something out. We might be lost, but at least we don't have that ugly white ape to worry about."

A surge of relief swelled through my body. Isaac was right. We were going to be okay. Yes, we were lost, but our snowshoes were still in the cabin, so we could get those back. And although the ice beast had broken down the front door, the building still provided shelter. We could start a fire in the fireplace and stay warm. By nightfall, I was sure that my parents would call the police, and they would send out search teams. It wouldn't be long before we were found.

Isaac began the tedious process of climbing down the tree, and I followed. We had to go slowly, because our bulky clothing kept catching on branches.

And I paused every few seconds to look

down at the ice beast below us in the snow. I didn't even want to get close to him.

Good thing he's dead, I thought.

Then, I thought of something else.

"We're going to be famous," I said to Isaac.

He held onto a branch and paused, looking at me through the limbs.

"How so?"

"Think about it," I said. "Not only do we have proof that the ice beast exists, but we actually killed the thing. And we're just a couple of kids."

"Yeah," Isaac said. "I guess you're right. That's pretty cool, when you think about it."

We continued our descent. Finally, I was on the last branch. I let go and dropped into the snow only a few feet from the dead creature. Isaac also dropped down, and we stood next to each other, staring down in wonder at the motionless ice beast.

"Man," Isaac said. "He sure is huge."

"Yeah," I replied. "He sure is."

I had been nervous about getting close to

the giant monster, but now I felt better. Now that the ice beast was dead, I wasn't so worried.

"Hey!" I said. I dug into my coat and pulled out my phone. "My phone has a camera! I can take a picture!"

"Great idea!" Isaac said. "I'll pose!"

Isaac moved closer to the ice beast, raised one foot, and placed his boot squarely on the creature's chest. He raised his arms triumphantly and smiled.

I held out the phone and looked into its viewfinder.

"Okay," I said. "Hold it there. It's focusing."

And that's when the ice beast moved.

21

The ice beast raised his arm. The movement caught us so off-guard that Isaac and I just stood there, staring in disbelief and amazement.

Very quickly, the initial surprise wore off and was replaced by a feeling of complete horror.

"He's alive!" I shouted. *"The thing is still alive! Let's get out of here!"*

Isaac pulled his foot from the ice beast's chest, and we began trudging through the deep snow back to the cabin. I kept looking over my shoulder, looking back at the ice beast. He hadn't gotten off his back, but he was still stirring.

He was only knocked unconscious, I thought. *The fall hadn't killed him after all. It had only knocked him out.*

Once again, our trek through the snow was maddeningly slow. Every step took an extra amount of effort, but we finally made it to the cabin.

I turned around and looked at the ice beast. He raised his arm again, but he still hadn't gotten up.

He's still dazed, I thought. *Maybe he'll be confused when he wakes up, and that'll give us time to get away. Maybe he'll forget about us altogether.*

We trudged around the cabin. The front door was completely knocked off its hinges and lay in pieces inside the cabin.

"Let's get our snowshoes on and get out of here," Isaac said.

"But where are we going to go?" I asked.

"Doesn't matter," Isaac said, and he hurried

through the front door. "We're not safe in the cabin, we're not safe in a tree. That thing might come after us, but if we have a good head start, maybe we can find a trail. If we can find a trail, we can find other people that might be able to help us. My map says that all of the trails are well marked, so we should be able to make our way back to the main lodge."

While I wasn't sure if Isaac's plan was the best thing to do, I realized that he was right. As long as we were in the woods, we were in danger. If we could make it to a trail, I was certain that we'd be able to find our way back to the resort.

I followed Isaac into the cabin, found my snowshoes, and quickly strapped them on. We left the cabin.

"I say we go that way," Isaac said, pointing. "From where we are right now, the ice beast can't see us, because we're on the other side of the cabin. Let's head in that direction and hope we can get out of sight before he starts after us."

"Maybe he won't come after us at all," I said

as we started our trek. With the snowshoes on, it was much easier to walk, and we were able to move much faster.

"Maybe the fall from the tree stunned him," I continued. "Or maybe he'll think that we're not worth the effort."

"Or maybe he'll be madder than ever," Isaac said.

From behind us, we heard a long, horrible roar that caused us to stop in our tracks for a moment. Then, we kept on trudging over the snow, faster than ever, searching for a trail and trying to put as much distance as we could between us and the ice beast.

But that roar bothered me a lot. That wasn't the roar of a creature that was mad. That was the roar of a creature that was *furious*. Something told me that our troubles with the ice beast were far from over.

And very soon, I would find out that I was right.

We continued walking, and the minutes ticked by. It had finally stopped snowing, and I didn't know if that was a good thing or not. The heavily falling snow made it difficult to see, which meant that it helped to hide us from the ice beast, if only a little. Now, we were out in the open, moving through the forest in plain view of anyone or anything.

But we hadn't heard anything else from the ice beast, and our frequent glances over our shoulders detected no sign of the creature. With every step of my snowshoes, I became more hopeful.

Maybe we're going to get away, after all, I thought.

But we still hadn't found a trail. While we walked, Isaac dug out his map, trying to make heads or tails of where we were.

"I still can't figure out where we are," he said. "But sooner or later, we have to come to a trail. There are lots of them that crisscross through the forest."

"I hope you're right," I said. "I'm getting tired."

Every so often, we stopped to listen, hoping to hear the sound of people or perhaps the mechanical sound of a chair lift in operation. We heard nothing but silence. The wind wasn't even blowing, and there was no whisper from the trees.

And that began to bother me.

Things began to seem too quiet, too still, too peaceful. It was as if it was the calm before the storm, the minutes just before the lightning ripped open the sky and thunder boomed and growled with all its fury.

"Do you feel that?" I asked Isaac.

"Feel what?" he asked. "Tired?"

"No," I said, shaking my head. We continued walking, but I kept turning my head, staring into the forest around us. "I'm just getting a strange feeling."

"I don't feel anything," Isaac said. "The only thing I feel is the cold air on my face. The rest of me is plenty warm."

"No, not that," I said. "But look around. The wind isn't blowing, the trees aren't moving, and everything is silent. It's almost as if it's *too* quiet."

"It's just your imagination," Isaac replied. "Actually, I'm glad it's quiet. That makes it easier for us to hear other people or maybe a chair lift or the honk of a car horn from the resort parking lot."

"Yeah, you're probably right," I said.

We pressed on. I was still bothered by the eerie calm, but I didn't say anything more about it. The terrain changed, and we encountered some large boulders and passed by several cliffs. It was difficult walking up and down the steep hills, but the snowshoes made it easier. Every time we found a ledge or a hilltop, we walked to it and looked out at the distant mountains and deep valleys hoping to see the ski hills or maybe the resort itself. We saw nothing but the vast wilderness, and although I knew we were only a couple of miles from the town, it appeared as if we were thousands of miles from civilization.

And every few minutes, I pulled out my phone, hoping to have a signal. There was none. I hadn't received any calls or text messages, and when I tried to send a text to my dad, it didn't go through.

We stopped at another ledge and looked out, but we saw no signs of the resort or the ski hills. Below the ledge was a steep drop off with deep, powdery snow. Rocks and boulders jutted out in several places.

"At least that thing isn't following us," Isaac said as he glanced behind him, down the slope. "I hope he found better things to do."

Isaac was right: the ice beast wasn't following us . . . he was much smarter than that, and he was certainly smarter than I'd given him credit for.

Which is the reason why I was disturbed by the stillness of the forest and the hills. It was too quiet, too calm, and it was no surprise when I looked up to the right of us and saw the ice beast partially hidden behind a large boulder, watching us . . . .

I stopped in my tracks and grabbed Isaac's arm. He stopped, too, and I pointed ahead with my gloved hand.

"Isaac!" I hissed. *"Look!"*

He knew what he was doing, all right. He had circled around the other side of the hill and was stalking us. He knew that if he followed us, we would be looking for him, so he had circled ahead of us and waited for Isaac and me to come to him. He had laid a trap for us, and it had worked perfectly.

Worst of all, we were standing on a rocky ledge. It was like being in the tree again: there was nowhere to go. Unless, of course, we jumped off the cliff, which I was certain would mean instant death.

"This is like a nightmare that I can't wake up from," Isaac said.

"It's a nightmare, all right," I agreed, "but trust me: you're awake, because I'm experiencing the same thing you are."

For the moment, it was a stare-down. We looked at the ice beast, and he continued to watch us. He simply stood there, breathing, snorting his frosty breath like a horse.

I looked around. Our only escape route would be down the hill, back the way we came. Even then, it wouldn't be an escape, as I was sure the creature would quickly overtake us.

And behind us? The ledge. I looked down at the snow and rocks some thirty feet or so below.

Not a chance, I thought. *We can't jump.*

The ice beast began to move. His motions were slow and deliberate, and he appeared to be sizing us up, as if he was wondering about the best way to reach us without us getting away.

Then, the creature stopped. He turned and faced a large shelf of rock. At the base of the stone, snow had melted in a large crevice, creating a thick block of ice. While we watched, the ice beast reached out and punched the ice with one enormous fist. A chunk of ice the size of a garbage can broke off, and the beast picked it up with ease and raised it over his head.

Isaac spoke. "What's he going to do with—"

He never had a chance to finish his sentence. The creature used the block of ice as a weapon, hurling it at us. It became a deadly torpedo, a massive missile on a direct collision course with Isaac and me . . . and there was nothing we could do about it.

Isaac and I tried to dart to the side, but we weren't fast enough. The huge ice boulder struck Isaac on the arm and spun him around. I was struck just above the waist, but luckily, I was caught only by a corner of the projectile. It knocked me over, and I nearly fell off the cliff, but the ice block hit the edge of the ledge, broke in two, and vanished over the edge, tumbling into space to smash on the rocks below or plunge into the deep snow.

The ice beast raised his hands in the air,

tilted his head back, and let out another ferocious snarl. His breath emitted a foggy cloud.

Isaac scrambled to his feet and almost tripped over his own snowshoes.

"We don't have any choice!" he shouted. "We have to jump!"

"Are you nuts?!?!" I replied, glancing behind me at the steep drop-off. "We'll get smashed on the rocks!"

"It's better than being torn apart by that thing!" Isaac said. "Besides: if we can jump far enough, we might not hit the rock ledge. We might land in the snow. I'm sure it's deep enough for us to jump into without getting hurt too badly."

Too badly. I thought about those words. That meant broken legs, arms, ribs . . . any number of serious injuries. Actually, it was a miracle that we hadn't been hurt already. We could've fallen from the tree or been ripped to shreds by the ice beast. We'd been lucky . . . but it appeared that our luck was about to run out.

Isaac fell to the ground and began

unstrapping his snowshoes.

"Take your snowshoes off!" he said. "You'll be able to jump farther without your snowshoes on!"

I fell to the ground and quickly unstrapped the snowshoe harnesses. Isaac had already tucked his snowshoes beneath his arm and stood.

Meanwhile, the ice beast was coming toward us. His attempt to hit us with the block of ice had failed, and now he was storming up the hill.

And he wasn't moving slowly, either. The snow wasn't very deep at all, and where we stood, there was no snow at all. He bounded up the hill with surprising speed.

"Jump as far out as you can!" Isaac ordered. "Try to land in the snow!"

I looked over the edge of the cliff, at the snow and jagged rocks below.

There's no way, I thought. *I'll never jump far enough to land in the snow. I'm going to hit the rocks for sure.*

Isaac sensed my fear and held his gloved

hand out.

"We'll jump together," he said. "Hurry! We don't have much time left!"

I held my snowshoes beneath one arm, and with my free hand, I grabbed Isaac's hand. We didn't even wait to count to three. We took two steps back, then leapt forward. I kicked as hard as I possibly could, thrusting myself over the ledge.

Then, we were in the air, falling down, down farther, faster and faster. The farther we fell, the closer the rocks came, and I realized at the moment before we hit, that we hadn't jumped far enough.

Everything was black—but I was alive. I was alive, but my face was cold and wet.

Slowly, I raised my arm. Then, I moved my leg.

"Jessica?" Isaac asked. His voice was muffled, and he sounded like he was a few feet away.

I wiped my glove over my face and opened my eyes to a gray, cloudy sky.

"I'm okay," I said, surprised and amazed to

hear my voice. I stood, but the crazy thing was, the snow came up to my shoulders! That's why we survived the fall.

Isaac was nearby. His hair was all askew and filled with snow.

"Are you all right?" I asked.

"Yeah," he said. "But look."

He pointed. I turned around to see an enormous boulder only a couple of feet away. We had just barely missed it. I don't know how, but we had leapt far enough that we had made it over the boulder and landed in the deep, soft snow.

"Let's get our snowshoes on and get moving," Isaac said. "There's no telling what that thing is going to do next."

We looked up to see the enormous ice beast standing on the ledge, staring down at us. Just for fun, I stuck out my tongue at him. I know that it was silly, but it made me feel better.

I had lost my snowshoes in the fall, but they were easy enough to find. It was a struggle to put them on, because the snow was so incredibly deep.

But I sure was glad I had them. If we didn't have snowshoes, there was no way we would be able to walk at all. Not in snow that was up to my shoulders!

Once we got our snowshoes on, we were able to walk over the snow. We sank down a little bit, but it was still relatively easy to walk, and we began to head down the mountain, weaving around rocks and boulders.

"I hope that's the last we see of that creature," I said.

"Me, too," Isaac said. "Hey," he continued. "Check your phone to see if you have a signal."

I dug into my right pocket, then my left. Suddenly, I was stricken with a sickening feeling.

I stopped, unzipped my coat, and searched my inside pockets. Nothing.

"What's wrong?" Isaac asked.

"My phone!" I said. "I lost it!"

"Probably when you landed in the snow," Isaac said. "Well, we can't go back now. Besides, even if we did, it would be impossible to find it in snow so deep."

He was right. I was just going to have to face the fact that the phone was lost, that our last hope of communication was gone.

"My parents are going to be mad," I said as we started out again.

"I think once your parents find out what's happened to us, they'll just be glad that you're still alive. I don't think they're going to be too worried about you losing your phone. Phones can be replaced."

"You're forgetting one thing," I said.

"What's that?" Isaac asked.

"We still have to get back to the resort. We're still lost, and we're far from safe. And that thing is still out there, somewhere."

"Try to look on the bright side," Isaac said. "We've gotten away from the ice beast three times now. He might still be after us, but he'll have to take the long way, back around the other side of the hill."

We trudged on. Above us, the gray clouds

were breaking up. We began to see blue sky and trickles of sunlight. Even with the seriousness of our situation, I looked around and realized the perfect beauty of our surroundings: the trees; the snow; the clean, cold air. Idaho sure has some beautiful places.

But it was at the top of the next hill that we spotted something that caused our hopes to soar.

A couple of miles away, down in a valley, we spotted what appeared to be the resort and the town of Sun Valley.

"There it is!" I yelled. "There's the resort! There's Sun Valley!"

"We're home free!" Isaac shouted.

Well, not exactly. The ice beast wasn't going to give up so easily, as we were about to find out.

"I'm surprised we're so far away from the town," I said as we continued onward. "We must be two miles from the resort."

"It shouldn't take us long to reach it," Isaac said. "Now that we know exactly what direction to head, we don't have to worry about getting lost again."

Moments before, while we stood looking at the distant resort, Isaac had taken out his emergency survival kit and withdrawn the small compass. He looked at it to get his bearings, so that we'd know in which direction to head if we lost sight of the town.

"I'm glad we finally found it," I said. "I'm getting hungry, and we fed all of our food to that crazy polar orangutan."

Isaac laughed. "Polar orangutan," he said with a chuckle. "That's funny."

We were feeling good. We didn't feel so helpless and hopeless, now that we knew in which direction the resort was. In an hour, we would be safe inside the lobby, seated by the fire, relating our incredible experience to my family.

"It's too bad we weren't able to get a picture," Isaac said. "I wonder if anybody's going to believe us."

"My parents know that I don't lie," I said. "They'll believe me. And they'll believe you, too."

"You know what else is funny?" Isaac said.

"What?" I replied.

"Thousands of people have spent years looking for the ice beast, Bigfoot, Sasquatch, the abominable snowman, whatever you want to call him. We actually found the creature and can't wait to get away from him!"

I laughed. Isaac was right. We'd experienced something that so many people had wanted to experience. So many people wanted to be the first to discover the creature, to prove his existence, and it turned out that he was discovered by two kids on snowshoes that just went out for a simple trek through the forest.

But I had to admit: I was very tired. My legs felt heavy, and my muscles were sore. I wanted to stop and rest, but I didn't think it would be a good idea.

Every once in a while, Isaac looked at his compass to make sure we were headed in the right direction. He wanted to make sure we didn't veer off course, which would make our hike back to the resort even longer.

Finally, it was Isaac who had the idea to stop and rest for a moment.

"Let's take a break," he said as we

approached a fallen, dead tree. "I don't want to stop for too long, but I've got to rest."

"Me, too," I said. "My legs feel like rubber."

"I think we're about a mile away," he said. "We should be back at the resort within twenty minutes."

We took a seat on the fallen tree. It was good to relax and take the weight off my legs. And it didn't help that I was very hungry. If I'd had food in my stomach, I probably would've had more energy.

After a few minutes, Isaac stood.

"Okay," he said. "Let's get moving. I can't wait to get a hamburger or a hot dog from the restaurant."

"I could eat an entire pizza," I said. And I meant it.

Thankfully, there had been no sign of the ice beast. We certainly hadn't forgotten about him, and we were constantly on the lookout, but after a while, we figured that he must have decided to leave us alone. Maybe he was just trying to get us out of his territory. Now that we were farther away, he wouldn't bother us.

But danger still lurked, unseen and unknown to us, on the other side of a thick spruce tree. As we hiked around it, we heard a noise and saw a huge, dark shape.

When Isaac and I realized what it was, we froze.

It was a black bear, and he was no more than ten feet from us!

The bear was facing the other way, and I was certain that he hadn't spotted us yet. Isaac and I stopped, frozen in terror.

I was surprised to see the bear, as most of them hibernate during the winter. However, I had read that once in a while, bears will get hungry and leave their den in search of food. That's probably what this bear was doing.

And we were too close to do anything. If we moved, the bear would most certainly hear us. The only thing we could do was stand there, motionless, hoping he would go away on his own without noticing us.

While we watched, the bear seemed to be eating something, but I didn't know what. I was just glad that it wasn't us!

And just when I thought he was going to wander off, he turned and saw us.

I tried to remember everything I had read about bear encounters, about what humans should do if they are attacked by bears. I'd read that it was best to play dead and not to move. If the bear thought you were dead and were no longer a threat, it would go away. I'd heard about several people who had done this, and it had saved their lives.

So, I was ready to drop down and crouch in the snow, ready to cover my head with my hands to protect it. I knew that at any moment, the bear could charge.

Instead, after his initial look of surprise wore off, he looked curiously at us, then turned and charged off into the woods.

"Whew," I said. "That was close. My dad says one of the worst things you can do is surprise a bear."

"I'm glad he just decided to run away," Isaac said. "Man! Between ice beasts and bears, we've had enough adventure in one day to last us for years."

"Let's just hope that was our last scare," I said. "I don't know what's worse: my tired legs or my growling tummy."

Isaac checked his compass again, and we kept going. We walked for only a couple of minutes, and Isaac suddenly stopped.

"Jessica," he said, "tell me that was your stomach."

I look at him, puzzled. "What do you mean?" I asked.

"That growling," he said, suspiciously searching the woods. "Tell me that was your stomach growling."

I shook my head. "I didn't hear anything,

and it wasn't my stomach."

Now, both of us were searching the forest around us, peering around tree trunks and through branches. The sun was shining and the white snow was very bright, in contrast to the shadows created by the trees.

Suddenly, we both heard it: a low, deep growl. But we couldn't tell where it was coming from.

"Do you think it's the bear?" Isaac asked.

"I don't think so," I said, shaking my head. "I think that bear got scared off by us. If you ask me, that sounds like—"

It was.

The ice beast.

He emerged from behind a clump of small pine trees and stood, watching us.

And he looked madder than ever.

While the creature stood watching us, Isaac took a
few steps to the left.

"What are you doing?!?!" I asked. *"We need
to run and get out of here!"*

"If we keep trying to outrun him," Isaac said,
"sooner or later, he's going to get us. We're both
too tired to try to run from him."

I still didn't understand what he was doing
as he bent down and picked up a dead tree branch.
Dead brown leaves filled the limbs.

" You're going to try to fight off the ice beast with a dead branch?" I said, glancing at the creature.

Thankfully, for the time being, he was just watching us, but I knew from previous experience that he wasn't going to stand there for long. It was going to be only a matter of seconds before he attacked.

"You'll see," Isaac said. Working quickly, he pulled out his emergency survival kit. He opened it and pulled out the box of waterproof matches.

The ice beast began to move toward us.

"I don't know what you're doing," I said, "but you better do something fast! He's coming toward us!"

Isaac managed a quick glance at the creature as he pulled a match from the matchbox. He struck it against the side of the box and a yellow flame flared. Then, he lit the dead leaves on the branch. The flames grew around the limb as the dry tinder caught. Soon the entire branch was aflame.

The beast kept coming, moving faster with

every step.

Isaac stood, holding out the flaming tree branch, and the effect was immediate.

The ice beast stopped.

Isaac shook the flaming branch toward him.

"Go on!" he shouted. "Get out of here! Go away, and don't come back!"

The ice beast cocked his head and looked puzzled.

Bravely, Isaac took a step forward, then another, and another.

"What are you doing?!?!" I asked again.

"I told you," Isaac said, still focused on the ice beast. He slowly waved the burning branch back and forth. The flames rose up; smoke filled the air. "We can't run anymore," Isaac continued. "We have to be smart. Maybe we can't fight him, but maybe we can scare him away. Most animals don't like fire, and that's what he is: an animal. Just what kind, I don't know."

I had to admit: it was the bravest thing I've ever seen anyone do in my life. The ice beast was three or four feet taller than Isaac and probably weighed as much as a cow or a horse.

Finally, when Isaac was only a few feet from the savage creature, he stopped.

"Jessica," Isaac said calmly. "Find another dead branch with dead leaves. This one isn't going to burn forever. But it's working. I think he's afraid of the fire."

I turned and looked in the area where Isaac had found the branch and quickly found several more. I had to break them from a fallen, dead tree, but I managed.

When I turned back around, the ice beast had taken several steps back, and he wasn't happy about it. He still looked angry, but clearly, he didn't like the fire. He was afraid of the flame.

"Let's go," Isaac said. "We'll have to walk and carry a burning branch with us to keep him away. As long as we have fire, I don't think he'll attack us."

The ice beast took several more steps backward.

"But what do we do if we can't find more dead branches?" I asked.

"We're both going to have to keep our eyes out for them," Isaac replied. "I'm sure dead branches won't be too hard to find in the forest."

So, that's what we did. We started out again, hiking across the snow, heading toward the resort. While we walked, Isaac carried the burning branch. When it had nearly burned itself out, I gave him another one, and he used his branch to light that one.

The problem was, the ice beast continued to follow us. He kept his distance, and he didn't come any closer, but he clearly wasn't going to leave us alone. If he had a chance, he would attack us.

His chance came, unexpectedly, as we tried to make it through a small ravine.

Isaac was right: we didn't have any difficulty finding dead branches to burn. Some of them were smaller than others, but the effect was the same. The ice beast stayed away. Yes, he continued to follow us from a safe distance, but he was fearful of the fiery branch. The problem came when we had to cross through a ravine. Here, the area was a little more open and there weren't many trees growing because of the vast number of rocks and boulders. We came to a place that looked as if it had once been a river, and the wind had blown most of the snow away. What was left was a trough of sorts, filled with uneven rocks, stones, and boulders of all different sizes. Walking across the ravine on our snowshoes was going to be difficult.

We stopped at the edge. Isaac held the flaming branch high to let the creature know who was in charge. I'd found four more dead branches, and I carried them in my arms.

"This is going to be tricky," Isaac said. "I think the best thing to do is take our snowshoes off and carry them through the ravine. There's more snow on the other side. We can strap on our snowshoes on the other side of the ravine and keep going."

That seemed like the best idea. The fire was working, keeping the ice beast away, so if we had to pause for a moment to take off our snowshoes, we weren't going to be in any danger . . . as long as the branch remained lit.

I unstrapped my snowshoes, and Isaac began

working at his with one hand, careful to hold the burning branch high with his other hand.

What happened next could have been prevented if we had only thought our plan through a little better. But my mom always says "hindsight is twenty-twenty." Twenty-twenty is what eye doctors call "perfect vision." So the saying "hindsight is twenty-twenty" means that it's easy to look back on a mistake you made and clearly see how you made it . . . but it's too late to change it, because it's in the past.

What happened that I wished I could have gone back and changed?

I should have unstrapped Isaac's snowshoes for him. He had to hold the burning branch, which gave him only one hand. Unfortunately, he stumbled, and because he still had his snowshoes on, he couldn't recover his balance, and he fell headfirst into the deep snow on the edge of the ravine.

Which meant, of course, that the flaming branch went with him. The branch sank into the snow with a series of hisses and pops, and the flames quickly dwindled.

The ice beast had been following us and waiting for his chance to attack. Now, he no longer kept his distance. Seeing that the flames were no longer a threat, he seized the opportunity . . . and charged us.

"Isaac!" I screamed, and I leapt to help him up.

"Leave me!" he said. *"Give me another branch so I can light it before these flames go completely out!"*

Isaac was still in the snow, and he quickly pulled the branch up. There were only tiny trickles of flame burning several small leaves; the snow had extinguished the rest.

Quickly, I held out another branch. The ice beast was still charging toward us, and he let out a roar that caused me to jump. I nearly dropped the branch I was holding.

I held the new branch against the rapidly diminishing flames. Several new leaves caught.

The ice beast kept coming.

The flames kept growing.

Isaac got to his feet.

As the flames bloomed, the ice beast slowed. He snarled and stopped only a few feet away, but as the fire consumed more and more leaves and the flames licked higher, the creature took a cautious step back, then another.

I heaved a sigh of relief, and my breath was foggy and gray for a moment before it dissipated.

"I'm sure glad you brought that emergency survival kit," I said. "I would have never thought of it."

"I just brought it because I thought it was cool," Isaac said. "I never thought we'd have to use it. Come on. Let's get to the other side of the ravine. We don't have far to go."

"But what if that thing follows us all the way

to the resort?" I asked.

"If he does," Isaac replied, "other people will see him. Then, everyone will have to believe us."

"But what if he hurts someone?" I asked.

Isaac thought about this as I picked up both pairs of snowshoes and tucked them beneath my left arm. In my right, I held three more dead branches.

"I don't think he will," Isaac said. "Remember: people have been looking for him, and creatures like him, for years. The reason no one sees them is because they stay up in the mountains and deep in the woods."

Carefully, we made our way down the rocky embankment through the belly of the ravine and up the other side. The ice beast followed us, and he had no trouble going around or over the large rocks.

When we'd made it to the opposite side of the ravine, we put our snowshoes back on. The creature snarled a couple of times and waited in the ravine. Once again, I was glad Isaac had thought about lighting the tree branch on fire. He had been right about the creature not liking fire, and his quick thinking had saved our lives.

But we weren't at the resort yet. We knew we were close, but the ice beast was still following us, even though he kept his distance. I wondered if we would encounter any other problems before we made it back.

"We're getting close," Isaac said. "I think I can hear the chair lifts running."

I turned to make sure the ice beast was keeping a safe distance, but I was surprised to see he had stopped and was looking up into the sky. He wasn't following us.

"Isaac, look," I said. Isaac stopped and turned around.

The ice beast was looking up, and he seemed confused.

Without warning, the creature began running, thundering off in the opposite direction.

"Weird," Isaac said. "What do you think caused him to do that?"

"I don't care," I replied. "But I'm glad he ran that way and not toward us."

We had just started out once again, excited that the creature was gone and we were only a few minutes away from the resort, when I heard a thumping sound. It was far away, but it quickly grew louder.

Isaac heard it, too.

"It's a helicopter!" he shouted. "Someone's looking for us!"

We stopped and scanned the skies. Suddenly, I saw it.

"Over there!" I pointed with the branches in my right hand. "There it is, right there!"

The helicopter was flying low, just above the treetops. Isaac waved the burning branch, but the helicopter was too far away to see us. Still, I was glad to know that someone was searching for us.

"That's what scared away that polar orangutan," Isaac said, and I smiled, secretly pleased that he had remembered my comment.

"Well," I said, "it doesn't really matter any

more. We're almost back to the resort."

Almost.

Yes, we were close.

But the ice beast wasn't done just yet. When the helicopter had flown over, the creature had run away to hide. Now that the helicopter had passed by, the giant monster was going to try one more time to get us before we could make it back to the resort.

And this time, he meant *business.*

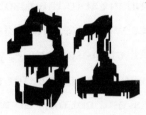

The first indication of trouble came from a noise ahead of us. At first, we thought it was a deer, but Isaac was the first to suspect that the ice beast hadn't run off after all.

"If he's in front of us," he began, "hiding in the woods, he's trying to block our way."

"But we have fire," I said confidently. "He's afraid of it. We should be able to get him to move out of the way."

Isaac had been right. The noise in the woods

ahead of us was the ice beast. He had been hiding in plain sight, kneeling near a large, bluish gray boulder. His white fur and ice blue skin blended in with the snow and rock.

And, as we suspected, he was going to try to keep us from making it to the resort.

"I wonder what we did that made him so mad," I said. "All of those people, year after year, searching the woods for proof, for any sign of the creature like this, and not only do we find one, but he attacks us and chases us down."

"Who knows?" Isaac said. "He's a creature nobody's ever studied before. Nobody knows anything about him or his behavior. We don't even know where he lives. All we know is that he exists."

We made a wide circle around the ice beast, but he moved closer. There was no question that he was going to challenge us.

So, that's what we let him do. We allowed him to get closer, knowing that he wouldn't approach us while we had the burning branch.

"Watch this," Isaac said with a grin.

The ice beast was about twenty feet away from us, and Isaac raised his voice and spoke.

"Hey, ugly! Where did you get those teeth? You really need to see a dentist! And that fur? Haven't you heard of a brush? You stink, too! You need a bath!"

Isaac snickered. I smiled, but I didn't know if it was smart to taunt the creature. Oh, I was certain the ice beast couldn't understand what Isaac was saying, but he might pick up on the sarcastic tone of Isaac's voice and know that he was being teased. I didn't think it would be smart to make him any madder than he already was.

"Oh," Isaac continued in his sarcastic tone, "one more thing. Why don't you—"

Isaac stopped speaking when I touched his arm.

"I don't think you should do that," I said to him. "He's already angry. We don't want to do anything to make him more mad at us."

"Don't worry," Isaac replied. "I've got the

fire. As long as I have this burning branch, that big fat polar orangutan isn't going to come near us."

Isaac was wrong.

Whether the creature understood Isaac or not didn't really matter. What the ice beast did understand was that Isaac was making fun of him.

And the beast didn't like it one bit.

Suddenly, he lunged for us, and the burning fury in his eyes told me that he was no longer afraid of the fiery branch. He was going to put an end to us, once and for all.

When the creature was only a few feet away and showed no signs of slowing, we knew we were in trouble. For whatever reason, the ice beast had decided he was no longer afraid of the fire. He was angry, crazed, and nothing was going to stop him.

But we had hesitated, and that, ultimately, is what saved us. We had waited, thinking that the beast really wouldn't attack. But he came toward us with such brute force and energy that, when Isaac went one way and I went the other, the beast wasn't able to change his course. He tried to grab both of us, but he missed.

However, he succeeded in splitting us up, and perhaps that's what he wanted in the first place. Perhaps he knew that together, we could outsmart him. But if he could get us apart, away from each other, he could hunt us down one by one.

I was so tired that my legs hurt, but fear does strange things to a body. When you know, without question, that you are in danger of being badly injured or worse, you somehow muster the energy to do things you never thought possible. I found myself running in my snowshoes, faster than ever, despite the fact that my legs were so weak I had thought I could hardly walk.

Meanwhile, the ice beast had stopped. Isaac was running in the opposite direction, away from me, and he was still carrying his burning branch. It was as if the monster was deciding which one of us to chase.

In the end, he must've decided that the fire

might be a danger to him, after all, because all of a sudden, he sprang in my direction.

I tried to run faster. I screamed for help, but I knew it wouldn't do any good. We were close to the resort, but not close enough for anyone to hear me.

"Jessica!" I heard Isaac shout. *"Run! Run as fast as you can!"*

I dared not look behind me, as I didn't want to stumble and fall. I needed to focus my thoughts and my energy on moving as fast as I could over the newly-fallen snow.

Behind me, I could hear the ice beast snorting as he got closer. I could hear his massive feet and legs smashing through the snow as he approached.

And then, the worst possible thing happened: I tripped. Actually, I was surprised I hadn't tripped earlier, as running with snowshoes is not an easy task, especially when you're being chased by a hideous ice beast.

I stumbled, flying forward and throwing my

arms in front of me to break my fall. As soon as I landed in the snow I rolled to the side, struggling to get up . . . but it was too late.

Suddenly, the ice beast was looming above me. It was the closest I'd been to him, and he smelled horrible. I nearly gagged.

Isaac was right, I thought. *He really does stink, and he needs a bath.*

"Jessica!" Isaac shrieked.

But I couldn't respond. I was too stricken with horror. And besides: what could Isaac do now? It was too late. We'd almost made it back to the resort. Our lives had been at stake several times over the course of the day, and I had really thought things were going to have a happy ending. I had really thought that within a few minutes, Isaac and I would be safely in the resort, filling our mouths with food and relating our incredible ordeal to anyone who would listen.

I realized then that it wasn't going to happen.

The ice beast stood above me, his foggy

breath disappearing in the cold air like smoke. His enormous chest heaved. His eyes burned with a fury and a rage I'd never seen before in any animal or human.

I closed my eyes and waited for the horrible pain that I knew was coming.

Seconds ticked by, and the waiting drove me insane. I knew the beast was going to attack; why didn't he just get it over with?

I opened my eyes.

The beast wasn't looking at me. His head was tilted back, and he was staring up into the sky.

"Jessica!" Isaac shouted again. Still, I didn't answer him. I didn't want to do anything to draw the attention of the ice beast, who now seemed focused on the sky.

In the next instant, I knew why. There was a faint thumping sound in the distance. The helicopter was returning!

If the ice beast wasn't afraid of fire anymore, he still didn't like the helicopter. He looked down at me as if to acknowledge that I had won and he had lost, but there wasn't anything he could do about it. He turned and crashed away, soon vanishing into the forest.

I could hear the helicopter approaching quickly, but the trees around me were tightly knotted together, and I never saw it pass by. Soon, the chopper blades had faded once again.

Isaac was quick to come to my aid. He ran up to me and knelt down.

"Jessica?!?!" he said frantically. "Are you okay? Are you all right?"

"Yeah," I said. "But for a minute there, I thought I was going to be snow monster food."

I hadn't noticed it, but the sky had clouded over again. Again, it began to snow. Big, fluffy flakes were falling all around us.

"I've had enough of this," Isaac said as he helped me to my feet. "Let's get to the resort. We won't be safe until we get inside the resort."

I wasn't going to argue one bit.

He checked his compass one more time, then pointed.

"We're only a little bit off course," he said. "The resort should be right over there, and it should be just a short hike through these trees."

Was I ever glad that he was right! When we stepped out of the forest and saw the sprawling expanse of the resort, the ski hills, the parking lot, and all of the people, I don't think I've ever been happier in my life. I was exhausted, I was starving, but I was alive.

Somehow, even in our tired state, we trudged our way to the ski rack area. By now, the snow was really coming down, just as hard or harder than it had earlier in the day. We took off our snowshoes and walked into the lobby.

"Who are we going to tell?" I asked Isaac. "We've got to warn people. We have to tell someone."

"Let's tell the resort manager," Isaac suggested. "When he finds out what happened, he'll probably call the police. They'll probably send out a team to search for the monster."

We went to the front desk and asked to see the manager. She appeared a moment later. She was a smiling, well-dressed woman about my mom's age.

"Can I help you?" she asked.

Isaac and I both started speaking at once, rapidly, and too fast to understand.

The woman laughed and held up her hands.

"Please, please," she said, very good-naturedly. "One at a time. What can I help you with?"

I looked at Isaac and gave him a nod, allowing him to speak.

"I know this is going to sound crazy," he said, trying to speak slowly and to contain his urgency and excitement. "But we've been chased around all day by the Idaho Ice Beast. He really exists! Not only that, he's not far from here at all! You have to warn everybody."

The hotel manager looked at Isaac, then looked at me. Then, she looked at Isaac again and burst out laughing.

"Not another ice beast story!" she exclaimed. "Every year, we seem to get more and more people who claim they've seen that silly creature."

"But we actually *saw* it!" I said. "We could have been killed!"

The hotel manager shook her head. "Oh, I'm sure you have a good story," she said. "Everyone does. I guess it's good for resort business, though. It brings in a lot of tourists who want to go looking for the creature. No one ever finds him, though. All they ever get are blurry photographs that don't really show much of anything. Most photographs that do show what appear to be a creature are obviously fakes."

"But we're not making this up!" Isaac insisted. "This actually happened to us! There was even a helicopter that was looking for us!"

"Young man," the hotel manager said. She was still smiling, but I could tell she was losing patience with us. "The helicopter is for tourists who want to see our beautiful town from the air. No one was looking for you. Now, I hope you're enjoying your stay here at the resort, but I don't have time for nonsense and stories about a creature that doesn't exist. If there is anything I can help you with, I would be glad to. But I am very busy, so if you don't mind, I need to get back to work."

And with that, the hotel manager smiled one more time to let us know she wasn't all that angry with us, then turned and walked back into her office.

"I knew we should've snapped a picture," I said.

"Hey," Isaac said. "You lost your phone, anyway. Even if you had taken a picture, we wouldn't have been able to show anybody."

We walked through the lobby toward the big fireplace.

"Let's get something to eat," I said. "If I don't get some food in my belly soon, I think I'm going to faint."

"Good idea," Isaac agreed, and we walked toward the restaurant.

Suddenly, a woman burst through the doors that led to the ski area. She was in such a rush that she didn't even see us and nearly knocked us over. Still, she didn't even pay attention. She ran straight to a couple of ski patrollers who were warming and resting by the fire.

"Please!" the woman said as she approached the patrollers. "Come quickly! You've got to help! It's my friend! I . . . I think he's dead!"

I looked at Isaac. Isaac looked at me.

Both of us were sure that the Idaho Ice Beast had just claimed a victim in Sun Valley.

Later, when we found out what had happened, we laughed out loud. I guess we probably shouldn't have, being that someone had been hurt, but it had nothing to do with the ice beast. The woman's friend had fallen and been knocked unconscious. He hadn't been seriously hurt and didn't even go to the hospital. Our imaginations had gotten the best of us, and we had thought the ice beast had killed someone.

And, try as we might, we couldn't get

anyone in authority to believe our story. But my mom and dad believed us, and Dad was able to get some of the resort workers to go with him to look for tracks in the snow. However, by this time, it had been snowing so hard that all of our tracks—and those of the ice beast—were gone. They searched into the evening in the area where we had spotted the creature, but no one saw anything unusual. Finally, they'd given up the search. By the time they did, I was in bed, sleeping. I was so exhausted that I had hit the sack hours before anyone else.

The rest of the week, Isaac and I hung out together. We talked about the ice beast a lot, but we didn't talk about the creature to anybody else. We quickly found that no one was going to believe us.

Except for one person.

His name was Ray Carter, and he was from Maine. We were skiing, and the three of us rode the chair lift up the mountain together.

"Hey," he said as he looked at Isaac and

then at me. "Aren't you the two kids who saw the ice beast?"

I looked at Isaac, and he looked at me. By now, word of our adventure had spread around the resort, and we had become accustomed to people laughing at us. But Ray seemed serious, and he definitely wasn't laughing.

"Yeah," I said. "But I don't expect you to believe us. Nobody else does."

"Oh, I believe you, all right," he said, nodding. "I know of stranger things that have happened."

"What could be stranger than an ice beast chasing a couple of kids through the forest all day?" Isaac asked.

"How about mosquitoes bigger than eagles?"

Again, Isaac and I looked at each other with expressions of disbelief.

"What?!?!" we said at the same time.

Ray nodded. "Of course, no one believes me, either. But it happened. It happened last summer in Maine, not far from where I live."

"Giant mosquitoes?" I asked. "Are you serious?"

Ray bobbed his head. "Absolutely," he replied. "I can tell you all about it on the ride to the top of the mountain."

"I've got to hear this," Isaac said.

"Me, too," I said.

"Okay," Ray said. "It all happened one day last July, when my friend and I went to look for an old, abandoned haunted house."

An abandoned haunted house? I thought. *Giant mosquitoes? This is going to be the craziest story I've ever heard.*

But as Ray told us all about his horrifying ordeal, I realized that maybe it wasn't so crazy, after all.

I also realized something else: Without question, Ray had experienced a terror unlike anything I had ever known . . . .

Next:

AMERICAN CHILLERS

America's #1 Series for MAXIMUM Chills!

#33: Monster Mosquitoes of Maine

Continue on for a FREE preview!

I might as well admit it now: much of what happened to me and my friend, Abby McClure, was all my fault. Our friends dared us to go to the haunted house at the end of Mulberry Street, stand on the porch, and take a picture for proof. We weren't scared, because Abby and I don't believe in ghosts. We didn't believe anything we heard about all the strange things that people say happened there over the years. Actually, I don't think there's any such thing as a haunted house, which is why I decided to take the dare. So did Abby.

But this story, of course, isn't about a haunted house. It's about insects—ordinary mosquitoes—and the horrifying thing that happened to us.

But I know what you're wondering, and you're probably snickering as you read this. You're probably wondering what could be so horrifying about itty-bitty mosquitoes.

Well, I'll tell you.

Nothing.

There's nothing horrifying about itty-bitty mosquitoes.

It's the *monster* mosquitoes I'm talking about. Just how big are they? Spread your arms as wide as you can. More.

Even *more.*

That's how big they are. Monster mosquitoes bigger than eagles and vultures. Some of them have razor-sharp stingers that are over two feet long.

Those are the mosquitoes I'm talking about. When they're wings flap and they're buzzing in the air, they sound like airplanes. Their bellies are big enough to hold gallons and gallons of blood that they've sucked from their helpless victims.

These are mosquitoes you can't simply swat at. You can't swish them away with a quick sweep of your arm. Bug spray? Won't work. They don't go away if you happen to hit one with the back of your hand. Matter of fact, if one of these monster mosquitoes gets close enough for you to swat it, it's already too late. Not for them . . . for *you*.

But if Abby and I hadn't accepted that silly dare, if we hadn't gone to the supposed 'haunted' house at the end of Mulberry Street, you wouldn't be reading this story. And Abby wouldn't be plagued by the nightmares she has just about every night.

And I would probably be a normal kid that went outside, went camping and hiking in the woods like other kid my age, without the slightest worry about something so pesky as a tiny mosquito.

But I know better.

My name is Ray Carter. This is my story. This is how Abby and I discovered the Monster Mosquitoes of Maine, and how we had to fight the toughest battle we'd ever faced . . . just to stay alive.

2

"You're a chicken, Ray, and that's all there is to it."

I rolled my eyes. "Hardly," I said. "There's just no such thing as ghosts, and that old house at the end of Mulberry Lane isn't haunted. Everyone just says that."

There were four of us that afternoon: my best friend Abby, Doug Palmer, and Eddie Grimes. Doug and Eddie live a few blocks away. And me? I'm Ray Carter. I'm twelve years old, but I'll be thirteen soon.

The four of us were seated on our bikes in the shade of a huge tree in the park, which isn't far from where we all live. We had been talking about the house at the end of Mulberry Street, which is about a mile away. For years, stories have been told about the old house being haunted. It's been for sale for as long as I can remember. The grass is overgrown, most of the paint has chipped away, and I have to admit: it really *does* look like a haunted house.

But that doesn't mean it's haunted, and it doesn't prove there are any ghosts there. As I've already said: I don't believe in ghosts, and neither does Abby.

And that's why Doug and Eddie dared us to go to the house and stand on the porch.

"Let's do it, Ray," Abby said. "Let's go stand on the porch. Nothing's going to happen."

"Fine with me," I said. "I'm not afraid of that old place."

"We'll follow you and watch," Eddie said.

"Why don't *you* guys join us on the porch?" Abby asked.

Doug and Eddie shook their heads.

"No way," Doug said. "That place gives me the creeps."

"Me, too," Eddie agreed. "Why, I heard . . . " And he spent the next five minutes telling us all about the horrible things that had happened there, all of the ghosts that haunt the house. Abby and I listened, and every once in a while we would glace at each other and roll our eyes.

After we finished, we began pedaling down the street, heading for Mulberry Lane. Abby and I were certain that we would prove Doug and Eddie wrong. We were certain there was nothing at that old house that could possibly freak us out.

Man, were we in for a surprise.

3

It took us less than ten minutes to reach the house. We turned into the driveway and rolled to a stop. Doug and Eddie hung behind us; they didn't want to get too close.

If someone were to pull up right behind us at that moment, they would have seen a curious sight: two rows of four bikes with me and Abby in the front, Doug and Eddie in the back, all peering up at the aging, two story home with the unmowed lawn and the blue and white 'for sale' sign planted in the front yard. The grass was so tall that the sign was barely readable.

Without a word, Abby and I slid off our bikes and gently laid them down on the cracked gray driveway.

Abby turned and looked at Doug and Eddie.

"Wanna join us?" she asked with a dry smile.

"Are you kiddin'?" Doug replied. "That place is haunted. I'm not getting near it."

"I wouldn't touch it with a ten-foot pole, Eddie said.

"Hey," I said, "you were the one calling me and Abby 'chickens.'"

"We've already been on the porch," Eddie said. "Last summer. That's when we saw the ghost in the window."

"He came after us," Doug said with a nod.

I rolled my eyes. "It was probably the reflection of a bird," I said.

"Believe what you want," Doug said. "The place is haunted. And I bet you can't stay sixty seconds on the porch before you both run away, screaming your heads off."

"Or maybe the ghost will get you," Eddie said.

"Come on, Abby," I said to Abby, in a low voice only she could hear.

Abby smiled, and together we walked up the driveway to the house, turning onto the cement walkway that led to the porch. Here, the weeds and grass had grown so tall that it bent over the narrow path like thin, green tongues, and the vegetation licked at our jeans.

"This place really needs a good mowing," I said. "Nobody's going to buy a place that looks this ugly."

"Maybe that's why it's been for sale for so long," Abby said.

I turned to see Doug and Eddie, watching us from their bicycles in the driveway.

Goofballs, I thought. *They actually believe in ghosts.*

We reached the porch and stopped. I had to

admit, the house *did* look a little creepy, with its paint-chipped siding and dirty, smudged windows. I stared into the living room window and imagined the image of a ghost staring back at me, waiting for me to get closer . . . .

"Well," Doug shouted. "Are you going to step onto the porch or just stand there staring?"

"Maybe you're scared," Eddie sang.

I frowned, and stepped up onto the porch. Abby followed. Then, we turned to face Doug and Eddie.

"Start counting out loud," I said loudly.

"One," Doug began, "two, three . . . ."

"This is so silly," Abby said. "They actually think this place is haunted. Too funny."

Then, Doug suddenly stopped counting. He was supposed to count to sixty, but he stopped at twenty-two. His jaw fell, and Eddie's expression was identical.

Without a word, Doug and Eddie spun on their bikes and began pedaling faster than I have ever seen them pedal in their lives. Soon, they'd crested the hill and were gone.

"What was that all about?" Abby asked.

I shrugged. "I have no idea," I said.

Then, we heard a slight squeak behind us. Abby and I turned and could only watch in horror as the old, decaying front door began opening all by itself!

Abby and I stood, our bodies immobilized by fear. While we watched, the front door slowly opened. Ancient hinges groaned and squeaked, and it sounded like the door was going to fall over . . . or fall apart right before our very eyes.

I was barely aware that Abby had grabbed my arm until her nails were pinching my skin. Even then, I couldn't do anything about it. I was too terrified by the opening door to do anything.

Then, a ghostly figure appeared. The dark silhouette of a man.

I had seen enough. I wasn't hanging around anymore, and I was just about to turn and run from the house when a voice spoke my name.

"Ray? Ray Carter? Is that you?"

I paused, looking at the man who emerged through the doorway. He looked a little familiar, but I couldn't be sure.

And he most definitely *wasn't* a ghost.

"Aren't you Ray Carter, Tony Carter's boy?"

"Yeah," I said, still a bit confused.

Abby was still squeezing my arm, and I shook it so she would release her grip. Her nails left red welts on my skin.

"I'm Mr. Henderson," the man said. "I'm the realtor who's listing your house."

Suddenly, I remembered him.

"Oh, yeah," I replied. "Wow! You sure scared us!"

"Sorry about that," he said as he closed the door behind him. "I have several listings on this street, and this is one of them. I come by once in a while to check on the houses."

Abby spoke for the first time. "But where's your car?" she asked.

Mr. Henderson pointed down the street. "A few houses down, parked at the McClutchey house. I just left it there and walked here. By the way," he continued, glancing at each of us, "what are *you* two doing here?"

"It was a dare," I replied truthfully. "Our friends say the place is haunted, and they dared us to stay on the porch for sixty seconds."

"Hahahaha!" Mr. Henderson said, throwing his head back. "You know, that old rumor about this house has been going on since I was a kid like you two. No truth to it at all. Fun to make up stories, though."

"We don't believe in ghosts," Abby said.

Mr. Henderson looked at Abby.

"Well, now," he said, frowning, "not so fast, not so fast. Don't be too sure of yourself. I used to think the same thing. But then, some friends and

I found the old abandoned Hooper farm a few miles from here. Saw some things there that curled our hair."

"Like what?" I asked.

"Oh, scary stuff," Mr. Henderson replied. "Ghosts, I guess. Not sure. But we saw things move on their own and heard strange noises, even during the day. We even went inside, once. Me and my friends, we got so scared we never went back. Ever."

I looked at Abby, and she looked at me. I knew she was thinking the same thing I was.

"Just where is this place?" she said, stealing the question right off my lips.

"Oh, about three, maybe four miles up the old power line trail. When you get to a big pond, you gotta turn right and head another mile. Can't miss the farm."

After a few minutes of chatting, Mr. Henderson left. Seated on our bikes, Abby and I watched him walk along the side of the road until he disappeared over the hill.

"I still don't believe in ghosts or haunted houses," Abby said.

"Me neither," I replied. "But I think it would be fun to check out that old farmhouse."

"Do you think he was just making it up?" Abby asked. "My uncle likes to make things up like that, just to fool kids."

"I know how we can find out," I said. "Let's go check it out ourselves."

That little decision was about to get us into big, big trouble. Trouble . . . with a capital 'M.'

ABOUT THE AUTHOR

Johnathan Rand has been called 'one of the most prolific authors of the century.' He has authored more than 75 books since the year 2000, with well over 4 million copies in print. His series include the incredibly popular **AMERICAN CHILLERS, MICHIGAN CHILLERS, FREDDIE FERNORTNER, FEARLESS FIRST GRADER,** and **THE ADVENTURE CLUB.** He's also co-authored a novel for teens (with Christopher Knight) entitled **PANDEMIA.** When not traveling, Rand lives in northern Michigan with his wife and three dogs. He is also the only author in the world to have a store that sells only his works: **CHILLERMANIA!** is located in Indian River, Michigan and is open year round. Johnathan Rand is not always at the store, but he has been known to drop by frequently. Find out more at:

www.americanchillers.com

ATTENTION YOUNG AUTHORS!
DON'T MISS

JOHNATHAN RAND'S

AUTHOR QUEST

®

THE DEFINITIVE WRITER'S CAMP
FOR SERIOUS YOUNG WRITERS ©

If you want to sharpen your writing skills, become a better writer, and have a blast, Johnathan Rand's Author Quest is for you!

Designed exclusively for young writers, Author Quest is 4 days/3 nights of writing courses, instruction, and classes at Camp Ocqueoc, nestled in the secluded wilds of northern lower Michigan. Oh, there are lots of other fun indoor and outdoor activities, too . . . but the main focus of Author Quest is about becoming an even better writer! Instructors include published authors and (of course!) Johnathan Rand. No matter what kind of writing you enjoy: fiction, non-fiction, fantasy, thriller/horror, humor, mystery, history . . . this camp is designed for writers who have this in common: they LOVE to write, and they want to improve their skills!

For complete details and an application, visit:

www.americanchillers.com

All AudioCraft books are proudly printed, bound, and manufactured in the United States of America, utilizing American resources, labor, and materials.

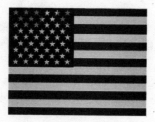

USA